PRAISE FOR
THE EXORCIST CASE FILES

"Benjamin Black's *The Exorcist Case Files* skillfully transports the reader onto the foggy, gaslamp-lit streets of Jack the Ripper's nineteenth-century Victorian London for an eerie, spine-tingling, and ultimately thrilling journey into the dark world of the occult. Evocative of Poe or Conan-Doyle, Black's riveting tale grasps the reader from the very first page like a possessive demon and won't let go. The only place to sit will be on the edge of your seat."

—Steve Jam, Author of *A Seventh Sense*, 2023 Winner of the Independent Press Award for General Fiction

"This book possessed me! With each chapter, I was hooked and couldn't escape the suspense and dark mystery. If you're a Constantine fan, you'll be a fan of this book too. Loved it."

—Denise Summers, Author of *An Immortal Sacrifice*

"This thrilling short work of fiction tells a tale of one who has been redeemed from a life of darkness yet now returns to it only to expose it. Set in Victorian England, the romantic and gothic intertwine, from a blossoming love story to hideous realities that only those led by unshakable faith would dare to face. Asher Grey is a must-read, and the story has only just begun!"

—Victoria P. Davis, Author of *Addicted to Health*

"Black's skill in penning this body of work evokes the same emotion I feel when standing before a great master's painting in which each brushstroke has been skillfully placed to create the whole. His storytelling is thought-provoking and thrilling."

—Anna Chambers, Author of *My Name Is Mom*

"Author Benjamin Black's *The Exorcist Case Files* takes you right into the midst of a dark London during one of my favorite periods of history: the Victorian era. This is a good read that will both set your nerves on edge and let you see things that may or may not be real. The book left me wanting more and coaxed me to explore the unseen world that we so often think is just imaginary. Enjoy."

—Robert Boysel, Reader

"What an exceptional first book by Benjamin Black! A genre of its very own! Thrilling and surprising, I could feel 1880s London [through the] vivid visualization in his writing. The author is also an excellent artist, and the inclusion of his work in this book richly adds to his story. Black plants intriguing facts about his lead character, hinting at many fascinating tales to come. *More* adventures with Asher Gray and Lady Victoria, *please!*"

—SRB, Reader

"This is fast-paced, page-turning gothic horror at its finest—and at its most wholesome. Fans of the macabre will cheer a surprise encounter with a certain American legend—and his pet *raven!* I can't wait to see what demonic forces Mr. Grey and Lady Kaylock battle next.
"Seriously couldn't put it down. Five stars."

—ES, Reader

The Exorcist Case Files

by Benjamin Black

© Copyright 2023 Benjamin Black

ISBN 979-8-88824-015-1

All rights reserved. No part of this publication may be reproduced, stored in a retrieval system, or transmitted in any form or by any means—electronic, mechanical, photocopy, recording, or any other—except for brief quotations in printed reviews, without the prior written permission of the author.

This is a work of fiction. All the characters in this book are fictitious, and any resemblance to actual persons, living or dead, is purely coincidental. The names, incidents, dialogue, and opinions expressed are products of the author's imagination and are not to be construed as real.

Published by

3705 Shore Drive
Virginia Beach, VA 23455
800-435-4811
www.koehlerbooks.com

THE EXORCIST CASE FILES

BENJAMIN BLACK

VIRGINIA BEACH
CAPE CHARLES

To my wife,
who could see better than she thought,
and far better than I could.

AUTHOR'S NOTE

This book is a work of fiction. Names, characters, places, and incidents are products of the author's imagination or are used fictitiously. Any resemblance to locales or persons, living or dead, is entirely coincidental.

The content, however, is based upon actual events that I could say have been both a blessing and a curse to me.

TABLE OF CONTENTS

Chapter 1: A Call to Bedlam 1

Chapter 2: Snarls in the Dark 11

Chapter 3: Unexpected Meeting at the Evening Star 21

Chapter 4: The Past and the Prophecy 31

Chapter 5: Consultation with the Doctor 41

Chapter 6: Coffee with an Old Friend 55

Chapter 7: To Seek Out a Cult 67

Chapter 8: Family Insights 85

Chapter 9: Snake Pit 97

Chapter 10: Provoking the Pentacle 109

Epilogue 123

CHAPTER 1

A Call to Bedlam

LONDON

October 27, 1886

There are many cases of which I could write and in which the Almighty has seen fit to call me to participate. My mind often reels at the enormity of situations and adventures that have come my way, and if I attempted to record them all, my mind, let alone my pen, would fail me.

However, as now I endeavor to chronicle my past, I wish to relate a selection of cases that I would consider some of the most notable. And so, I have elected to begin with a particularly wicked episode that began in the fall season of 1886 in my precious London.

I had become somewhat controversial within the lesser-known pockets of society over the last several years. Some opined that I was fixated upon all topics macabre and unnatural, while others spoke my name with bewilderment and unease. Largely, everyone believes me to be, in the best instances, at least a little mad.

How could they not? I was fast becoming an expert in a field little known in the circles of modern civilization, and cultivated minds always flee from the mysterious and unexplained.

I am an exorcist.

And when I use the term exorcist, I do mean literally. I deal in battling the infernal, the ghastly, and the darkened. I have been in this vocation ever since my brief stint with death.

Yes, I died. But that's a story for another time.

Needless to say, in working an occupation of this sort, I have acquired a vast menagerie of associates, contacts, and, even greater still, enemies.

It was on the cold night of the twenty-seventh of October that I received a rather urgent telegram from one such acquaintance, Miss Amy Church.

Miss Church was the niece of a former client of mine whom I had aided several years earlier in a brief yet untidy case concerning an impudent poltergeist. Now Ms. Church—or, more accurately, Nurse Church—was a hireling at the notorious Bedlam sanitorium south of London and had asked that I come to her with the utmost haste.

Fortunately, my residence lay not too far, so I bundled up in my thick, gray coat and hailed a cab. The journey was quick by hansom, and before I knew it, I was looking out the carriage window at the sinister facade of Bedlam.

There are many edifices around the globe that carry with them a keen personality of hostility, or even malevolence, as if the walls themselves would, at the first opportunity, swallow you up into outer darkness.

Bedlam was, by my account, one such place.

The dense English fog wrapped about the structure like a silvery blanket cradling a grotesque statue. Several of the lights within were lit, denoting the unusually late hour. The gaslights at the front illuminated the front doors with a golden waxy hue.

Stepping out of the hansom, I paid the cabby and slowly ascended the thick stone steps to the main entrance.

I noticed immediately that someone, or something, was watching me. Something wicked. I could not focus on the presence, but I knew it was evaluating me.

Since my subsequent return from the dead years ago, I have

noticed several things that have been altered—*enhanced*—in me. One of those articles is my awareness of things around me, both visible and invisible. This awareness, or what I like to call discernment, allows me to feel, and to a degree see, through the veil into the supernatural and spiritual. This endowment is difficult for me to understand, as it seems to come and go as it wills, but over time, I have learned to trust it.

The evil presence continued its analysis of me as I reached the wide, double-doorway entrance.

Here I was greeted by a nurse dressed in the white orderly uniform of her profession, wringing her hands nervously. The woman was unexceptional in appearance, with straw-yellow hair tied tightly in a bun. She exuded an anxious air, and her eyes seldom left her shoes.

"Miss Church?" I inquired.

"Oh, um, yes, sir," the woman stammered. "I am Nurse Amy Church. I expect you are Mr. Grey, sir?"

I nodded. "I am Asher Grey."

The nurse bobbed her head excitedly, twisting her hands even tighter.

"Mr. Grey, thank mercy you've arrived. The doctors have tried everything, and all attempts have failed. Then, some of the most terrifying happenings began to occur, and all I could think of through the terror was to contact *you*, sir."

I raised one hand calmly, causing the frightened woman to pause in her tremulous blabber. She regarded me with wide eyes brimmed with tears.

"Breathe, Miss Church," I said softly. "Perhaps we should step inside and you can explain what prompted you to call upon me."

Nurse Church took a long inhale and timidly returned her eyes to her feet once again. "Yes sir. You're right, sir. This way."

I was led into a spacious main hall paneled in dark wood, with a high central staircase. To both my right and left were long hallways lined with doors. Even at this late hour, several orderlies patrolled the corridors. All of them appeared to carry a flavor of disquiet and uneasiness.

"May I take your coat, Mr. Grey?"

"Thank you, no. What is happening here, Miss Church? The dread is palpable."

The nurse directed me to the right, and we slowly made our way down the long hallway. Several lit candles and gaslights flickered, and the walls themselves seemed to dart about in shadow. Miss Church spoke as we walked.

"There was a patient admitted here. A Mr. George Brand. He has been with us these last six months, complaining of delusions and the belief that he hears voices.

"Does he?" I asked simply.

"Sir?"

"Does he hear voices?"

"If you would've asked me that question four months or even two months ago, I would've recommended that you be committed here, sir."

"But now?" I asked. "What has changed?"

A shrill cry rang out to our immediate left. Springing rapidly to push Miss Church behind me in protection, I quickly realized we were not in immediate danger. A patient wrapped tightly in leather straps and harness was crying out in anger as several large orderlies wrestled the poor wretch to his bed.

"This is commonplace at Bedlam, Mr. Grey," Nurse Church stated from behind me. "So, so many lost souls."

I relaxed a bit and resumed my place next to the woman as we continued our walk down the corridor.

"Please continue," I said.

"Yes. Over the last two months there has been a ... change in Mr. Brand's behavior. It began subtly, an outburst here or there, or bouts of depression and isolation. The doctors believed he was beginning to devolve into his psychosis."

"But something happened. Something that changed their minds," I whispered.

The nurse stopped abruptly. A nearby candle danced its light across her face as she looked at me.

"One night, I stepped into Mr. Brand's room to check on him, as is my duty. The room was very dark—and, I quickly realized, very cold. I could see my breath, sir. I made my way across the room, believing the window had been opened, but I didn't make it that far."

Miss Church's hands were shaking now at her memories. I kept silent, waiting for her to continue. After a long pause, she spoke.

"I heard . . . a sound. At first, I believed it to be the creaking of the building itself. This old place settles from the wind from time to time. I looked in the direction of the noise: a black shadow crouched in the darkened corner. I could only see it as a pitch deeper in shade than the dark around it.

"'Mr. Brand?' I asked, 'Is that you, sir?'

"That's when I heard it again. The sound. This time, however, I recognized what it was. A *growl*. God help me, Mr. Grey, it was a low, guttural growl like nothing I've ever heard before. I think from the raw panic I took several steps back, and when I did, the thing—Mr. Brand—raised his head to look at me."

I stepped closer to the woman, grabbing her arm unconsciously. "What did you see?"

"Oh, Mr. Grey. It was awful. His eyes, they *glowed*, sir! Red lights, as crimson and bright as burning coals! I turned to flee, running back toward the door as quickly as I could. Mr. Brand, he . . . lunged at me, screaming like some horrible, wild beast. I dove through the doorway into the hall, believing him to be chiefly on top of me, but instead his door slammed behind me, followed by cackling laughter from within that I shall carry with me the rest of my life.

"Since that night, any doctor or nurse that has attempted to treat or even enter Mr. Brand's room is met with immediate violence or alarming, unexplained experiences."

I removed my hand from the woman's arm and nodded. I knew now what I was about to confront and quickly understood the fear that had gripped Bedlam.

"Phenomena such as objects moving of their own power, sounds like whispering, and candles lighting of their own accord?" I asked.

"Yes . . . yes, Mr. Grey. How did you know?" Miss Church asked in surprise.

"Miss, I think you'd better take me to Mr. Brand's room immediately."

"Yes sir. We must be careful. Mr. Grey, I'm afraid I haven't been forthright with you. The doctors here, as well as many of the nurses, do not agree with me that Mr. Brand is being influenced by something unnatural. If they discovered I summoned you here—"

"I understand, Miss Church. It's quite all right. Please, let's hurry," I insisted.

That Nurse Church had commissioned my assistance clandestinely was nothing new. Unfortunately, when you operate in my occupation, you are usually met with skepticism at the very least. I had learned a long time ago never to take it personally. When people are exposed to the supernatural, it tends to produce a reaction. To someone who prides themselves on reason, that exposure can have turbulent results.

As I followed Nurse Church down the gloomy corridor, it was difficult to keep my eyes from pursuing the shadows that flickered and danced around the random placement of candles. The hairs on the back of my neck stood on end as that oppressive sense of being watched prickled my senses. My discernment was ringing like a brigade bell, warning me of what lay ahead, but I had to press on.

The nurse and I reached the end of the corridor, which was completed by a set of stairs that led down into darkness. Miss Church took a nearby candle from its sconce and motioned to the staircase.

"This way," she whispered.

We had only descended a short distance before we came into contact with another nurse ascending the same way.

"Nurse Church?" the woman said, stopping suddenly with her own candle in hand.

"Oh, excuse us," Miss Church nervously replied. "I was just taking this gentleman to check the leaky pipes, Nurse Kincaid."

The woman Miss Church called Nurse Kincaid was older, with a hard bearing and deep lines etched on her face. She narrowed her eyes at me suspiciously. She must have been Miss Church's supervisor.

"Very well, Nurse Church," Kincaid said brusquely. "Carry on. But be sure the job is done quickly. It's after hours. Go on, then."

"Yes, mum. Right away," Miss Church replied with a quick curtsy.

We passed the supervisor and continued deeper into the sublevel of the sanatorium. Our footfalls echoed as the passage around us pressed in black on all sides.

When we reached the bottom, we were met by a solid metal door, which Miss Church produced a key to unlock. As she pressed the key in the mechanism and turned, she spoke softly.

"This is the isolation ward where we keep patients harmful to themselves and others."

With a solid click, the door opened, and we stepped inside a narrow hallway. The floor and walls were gray stone, and the air was dank and musty. Despite this, however, it was uncharacteristically cold—far colder than was natural.

Miss Church hesitated. Her breath quickened, visible as puffs of white from the intense chill.

"Miss Church," I whispered. "If you wish to remain, I can manage from here. It's all right."

The nurse gulped audibly and nodded down the passage ahead of us. Along the right side were several iron doors—neglected isolation cells.

"I'm sorry, Mr. Grey. I . . . I can't go back there again. My feet won't move, sir," she gasped.

I rested my hand on the terrified woman's shoulder, attempting to lend her my strength.

"It's quite all right. Which door is it?"

Swallowing hard again, the woman produced a key and handed it to me. She choked out, "The last door, sir. Oh, God bless, sir. Please be careful."

With a reassuring pat, I released her shoulder, took the key, and headed down the passageway. I saw my breath with every exhale, signaling the presence of an unnatural entity. Spaces have a tendency to lower in temperature when a spirit or malevolent being enters them. This was confirmation that I wasn't about to have dealings with a mere ward patient. Of course, I did not need the cold to tell me that. My discernment was sending wave after wave of needle-like sensations over my entire body.

As I reached the edge of Nurse Church's light, I touched the final doorway of the passage. Oppressive wickedness emanated from within, a heaviness that attempted to provoke panic in my heart. I inspected the small name card attached to the door: G. BRAND. Inserting the key into the heavy lock, I turned it, and a thick clack echoed within.

With a deep breath, I undid the latch and stepped inside.

CHAPTER 2

Snarls in the Dark

Eggs and decomposition.

The cell of Mr. George Brand reeked of it. More precisely, it was the odor of sulfur—a common occurrence when dealing with the infernal. With demons.

This is quite familiar for exorcists. We often must expel a malevolent spirit from some poor soul who has become inhabited by the foul creature. Exorcism is Greek for "outward oath" after all.

I had not been in Mr. Brand's cell five full seconds before my assumption that I had a demonic possession on my hands was confirmed. Accompanying the stench of sulfur was that same bitter cold from the outer passage. Within the cell, it had greatly magnified. It felt as if all warmth in the world no longer existed in that place.

I waited for my eyes to adjust in the pitch black.

As I waited, I made out faint scuffling and scratching of movement at the far corner of the room.

"Mr. Brand," I called out. "Mr. Brand, are you there? I have come to help you."

Another shifting sound, this time followed by a low hiss. It reminded me of the felines I heard behind my tenement at night.

Eventually, I made out vague shapes within the room. It was sparse, with only a small bed at one end and a table and chair. I could tell the bed was soiled grossly and in disarray, and the table and chair were both shattered across the floor.

"Mr. Brand," I called out again.

Another hiss answered me, slightly louder and more aggressive than before. This time, I determined that the shape huddled behind the bed was the source of the noises.

"Mr. Brand, I have been asked to help you, sir. The people here are quite worried about your well-being. My name is—"

"I know who you are, *exorcist*," interrupted a wet, raspy voice that I dared guess was not Mr. Brand's, although it came from the same mouth.

"I know who you are, Asher Grey. The one rekindled from doom," the voice said in a tone of raw hatred.

"Who are you?" I asked bluntly.

The form of George Brand shifted slightly behind the bed, a low rumble escaping from him.

"What do you want here, Asher Grey?" the voice said instead.

"If you know who I am, then you know why I'm here. Let George Brand go free."

Two eyes peered over the bed at me. They glimmered in the dark like those of some predatory animal. The thing inside of Mr. Brand growled threateningly.

"He is *mine*. You cannot have him," it said.

I pressed in all the same. "Tell me who you are."

Without warning, the entire room shook violently, the tremors passing under my feet. Then, in the gloom, I beheld the fractured parts of the table and chair, as well as the bed itself, levitate into the air. The room filled with floating debris, slowly drifting.

I stood my ground—not only because I had experienced this before but also because the demon had overplayed its hand; for at that moment, I realized what I was at odds with.

Through the cloud of debris, the form of George Brand catapulted toward me, screaming in a bloody, primal cry.

I braced myself, but I suspected that I would not be harmed—not if my deduction about this spirit was accurate. My suspicions were proved correct when Brand's form abruptly ceased its trajectory but a hand's breadth from my face.

This was the first time I had seen Mr. Brand. Wild, wavy, dark hair wreathed his unshaved face. He appeared to be a man of once noble bearing, perhaps even a gentleman, but was now a shell of his former self. He did not seem much older than I, but his features were sunken and gray. What stood out, however, were his eyes. They belonged to no human being. These eyes burned crimson and had the slitted pupils of a serpent.

Mr. Brand stood before me, snarling fiercely and gnashing his teeth.

Any standard human being with any sense about them would have turned on their heels and proceeded to flee. I had personally witnessed a notable Catholic priest outright faint at the manifestation of a demon that was nowhere near the equivalent of what writhed before me. I cannot speak to whether I have anything in the way of sense left. It may have escaped me long ago. Unfortunately, I *can* state with a fair amount of certainty that I'm indeed not a standard human being. I could never flee. Not from this.

I could tell you I stayed due to an immense reserve of valor, or that I was overwhelmingly jaded by my profession. The truth, however, is that facing malevolence is my calling. Regardless of my wants, mine is an irrevocable path leading to a destination as uncertain as the gloom from which Mr. Brand leaped upon me.

I leveled my gaze at the thing that was George Brand, careful to betray no outward sign of emotion.

"I know what you are," I asserted calmly.

For the briefest moment, the spirit controlling this poor, mangled man hesitated. The snarl caught in Mr. Brand's throat, leaving a solitary string of drool running from the man's cracked bottom lip.

With a whimper, Mr. Brand pulled his dirty hands close to his body and groveled. He hunched into a stooped position, almost fetal, then shuffled back into the dark corner, his face turned away and his back now to me.

"Pale . . . the pale," he mumbled nervously.

"Enough of this nonsense. Let George Brand go," I insisted.

"The . . . the king. The pale king."

I took an unconscious step forward. "What? What did you say?" I whispered.

Brand screamed suddenly, a wail equal parts torment and fear. His voice gurgled, then crackled hoarsely at the finish, dwindling.

I was becoming a bit annoyed.

"Tell me what you said, you odious thing!" I commanded.

Brand twisted and groveled, all the while keeping his face hidden from view, as if struggling to keep from answering me.

Finally, he spoke again, through gritted teeth.

"The Pale King. The Pale King," he moaned pathetically.

This time, I was sure I had understood the demoniac clearly.

The Pale King. It was familiar, but the details seemed to slip from my memory. One thing was certain, however: although I could not summon the memories of where I had heard the name before, I experienced a deep sensation of impending doom at the sound of it—and a cold itch on my back.

"The Pale King? Who is that? What about him?" I demanded.

"No!" Brand screamed back. "No! You cannot know! Leave me, Rekindled One! Flee from me before I rend your bones!"

Taking another step forward, I directed my gaze intensely upon Brand. "I do not like repeating myself. I told you once already that I know what you are."

The demonic Brand growled and hunkered lower, perhaps willing himself to shrink from view completely. I refused to waver.

"And knowing what you are, I also know what you will and will not do."

Taking one final step, I stopped within arm's length of Brand, kneeling to look at the tormented being.

"You're an imp-level demon of fear. You scare to intimidate and control. But that is all. Under all of that is a coward. Demons of fear do not fight."

Brand's growling ceased, and he stared upon me with one wide red eye over his hunched shoulder.

"You can no more rend me than I can fly," I finished with a wry smile.

Now, as an exorcist, I am privy to a great many things. I have witnessed atrocities most could not comprehend and seen wonders that would answer many a search for the divine. That being said, I am not infallible. Although I have experienced more than most, I am still very much human.

A thought occurred to me: all of the objects that had previously been levitating under Brand's power were now strewn about on the floor.

The demon within Mr. Brand began to laugh.

It started small, like the giggle of a mischievous child, then intensified, growing into an outright maniacal cackle. At that moment, I feared I had made an error in judgment. I slowly rose back to my feet. Brand's cackle continued rhythmically, like a loop recording on a music box.

All at once, it stopped.

"Asher Grey," Brand whispered.

His voice had changed. Oh, it was still a disturbing, unholy voice, a voice not at all his own. But now it belonged to something altogether different—something much more malevolent, much eviler. The raspy wetness was replaced by deep, hollow baritones, like something very large speaking from a great distance.

"Asher Grey," it said again, "you are an interesting one. We have watched you with much interest of late—the Rekindled One returned from doom."

I attempted to keep my voice from shaking as I replied, "And you are?"

"An emissary. An emissary of the Pale King."

"I see. Well, perhaps this king and I could be introduced. I have questions for him. However, on second thought, why don't you pass on a message to your master instead? Tell him he's not welcome here. If he attempts to enter this plane and cross the veil, I *will* stop him."

The demonic emissary within George Brand cackled again.

"You are no obstacle. You are but a pebble to be kicked aside by the mighty and terrible," it growled.

I would not be intimidated.

"Perhaps," I answered, "but even Goliaths are vulnerable to a small 'pebble.' Now let George Brand go and return to your master. Tell him this man and plane are off limits."

"Fool!" the voice screamed back. "Your skin will be flayed upon the Pale King's balefires!"

Before I could react, the creature leaped up from its crouched position and flung itself toward me at an inhuman speed. I fell backward, attempting to keep my legs between myself and the savage creature tearing at me. My back hit the floor hard, and I gasped for breath.

Brand was upon me then, his fingers extended like jagged talons for my throat. I brought my hands up with haste, scarcely avoiding the fiend's lashings as I held his wrists. His considerable strength tested the very limits of my own.

The demoniac's face but inches from mine, the infernal spirit inside screeched and screamed, causing the poor man's body to convulse and twitch while ever-increasing strength bore down upon me. Spittle from the devil's mouth dripped upon me from cracked lips and yellow teeth.

"In the name of God," I began through clenched teeth, "and his Son, and the most Holy Ghost, release George Brand this instant!"

The man tossed his head from one side to the other, straining to fight off an unseen force. He growled and gasped for breath, and in that instant, I felt his generous strength weaken slightly. I swiftly released one of his wrists and sent my hand to his forehead, my palm smacking against his pale, sweat-covered flesh and clutching Brand's skull.

Now, as I have alluded to, ever since my extraordinary and bizarre return from death, the Almighty has seen fit to bless me with several unusual boons. One such benefaction was that of the discernment I spoke of previously, but another, and perhaps the least understood of them all, is the ability to quite literally touch spiritual entities. How I am able, I am not sure, but it is as if my physical extremities come into bodily contact with the incorporeal and even interact with them.

As I grabbed George Brand's head, the demon inside jolted with the realization that I was grasping onto *it* and not simply the poor soul it was wearing. Its slitted eyes widened within the man's skull, and it wailed in indescribable anguish.

"Apparently, you did not watch me close enough, or else you would've known that you cannot hide from me inside some victim!" I exclaimed.

What I can only describe as blue-hued lightning danced down my arm and rippled over Brand's face and head. Energy surged from within me, directed into the demon. Brand's head and body bucked wildly as the entire tone of the battle between us now shifted. The spirit was straining with all its might to escape *me*.

I pressed in with even more fervor. Blue lightning crackled.

"I charged you to release George Brand. I have little regard for whose emissary you may be, Pale King or otherwise. If you will not expel yourself, then I will come in and drive you from your hiding place!"

I sat up against the demoniac, applying considerable pressure to the delirious man's forehead. The demon inside howled as it found itself being pushed out of George Brand's back.

The foul thing emerged as if from within a cocoon, grotesquely rising from the man's head and back with putrid green skin. It was a revolting, humanoid shape of a thing, crooked and bent as it clawed at the man's back to desperately pull itself back inside. Its red, slitted eyes were wide with shock and horror at the suddenness of having been countermanded.

"The . . . the Pale King," the demon wheezed desperately. "He . . . *will* crush—"

I sprang forward, extending my arm past George Brand's head and grasping the throat of the fiend solidly. Blue light skipped across its stunned face. The demon gurgled as its sentence was physically cut short.

"No," I interrupted. "Your master will do no crushing today. Now be gone from this man, and return to the abyss to be judged."

With an immense cry, the demon scraped at the air, frantic to remain on this plane. Its body gradually disintegrated—first its legs, then its torso and arms, and lastly its repulsive head.

In one last, tormented scream, the demon cursed my name and vanished from the physical world.

I dropped my head in equal parts exhaustion and relief and realized I was on one knee in a crouched position. I then noticed two bare, dirty feet before me. Raising my head, I found George Brand sane and in his right faculties, albeit a little confused. He extended his hand to me. I took it and pulled myself upward to stand.

The man looked around the cell as if waking from a long dream.

"Pardon me, sir," he said timidly in his own voice. "But might I ask where I am? I cannot seem to recall how I arrived here."

I smiled weakly and clapped one hand on George Brand's shoulder.

Turning my head, I yelled toward the door, "Nurse Church! Come in now, please! Everything is safe. Mr. Brand is no longer in any danger. The threat is over."

CHAPTER 3

Unexpected Meeting at the Evening Star

LONDON

October 28

S unlight is a remarkable thing.
   Taken for granted by so many, it is the condition under which most simply go about the mundane repetition of their existence. Few, save for the most desperate and destitute, seek comfort and solace from his radiance.

As I stepped out the front door of my tenement, one obvious quality of daylight's splendor grabbed my attention: the absence of darkness. Looking up and down Knight's Street, I saw only the bustle of morning traffic—the epitome of the British Empire. Londoners walked past me on the sidewalk, a hansom passed a cart of Haversham's cheese, and an elderly spinster shook out a rug upon her stoop across the street. There was only light, and no trace of the previous night's wickedness.

I started my morning quickly after a bit of toasted bread and coffee. There was much to do, and my mind was fixated upon the name of the Pale King. Although I was rested after my late excursion in Bedlam, I still carried that lingering sense of dread. It could not be shaken or dismissed, even in my precious sunlight.

Over the course of my considerable yet bizarre career, I have established many contacts, several of whom could be considered, at the very least, suspicious. Amid this list of unsavory contacts, one personage instantly came to mind as one who might educate me on the identity of the Pale King. He was expert in all matters occult, although not a little eccentric in his manner.

Standing along the street's edge, I hailed the passing hansom to make my way across London to this contact's residence. I gave the coachman directions and eased back in my seat as the carriage lurched into motion. The rhythmic clip-clop of the horses' hooves on cobblestones filled my ears.

I barely took notice as the hansom crossed Waterloo Bridge, my mind pulled inward. My years of dealing with the disturbing and unearthly had never led me to an exorcism of last night's type. There were always occasions for new experiences, but I was keenly aware that this signified something far more distinct and troubling.

The hansom wobbled onto Aldwych, turning left into the Strand. We would travel north into Charing Cross, where my unusual acquaintance had established himself in relative secret several years earlier. He despised sudden visitors, but I had a sneaking suspicion he would quickly forgive my intrusion at the revelation of what bizarre new issue I was visiting upon him.

Moving in our northern direction, I watched from the hansom window as the busy streets of London passed me by. There was a deep-seated affection buried within my heart for this growing sprawl. From the grandeur of the National Gallery to the business of the Hippodrome, London would first and always be my home.

The hansom clip-clopped into Cambridge Circus, an intersection of many avenues of business from virtually every level of society.

With a heave, the carriage came to a sudden halt. I heard the coachman yell, "Whoa! Eh?"

Parting the curtain on my window, I stuck my head out and addressed the coachman.

"What's the trouble?"

"Dees young buggers nearly got trampled on! Why don'tcha get a move on, ya little gits!"

I glanced up ahead of the hansom to see that a half dozen young boys, none over ten years of age, had darted into the street, causing the coach horse to frighten and buck. The coachman's irritation was considerable, but not without cause. I took a brief look at our surroundings and hopped from the carriage as a young boy scampered away under the coachman's assault.

"It's not a problem. We are very close. I can walk the rest of the way." I paid the coachman and trotted nimbly through the busy traffic of Cambridge Circus.

Nestled silently off the main avenue of Charing Cross Road lies the Evening Star, a specialty bookstore that seems to hide in the shadows of the larger buildings surrounding it. It is typically empty and quiet, with only a rare few patrons ever frequenting its door. I have often wondered how the proprietor finagles the finances to keep the old place open.

To my surprise, as I neared the oaken front door of the establishment, it burst open. A large man emerged with an air of what I immediately identified as vigilance. A bodyguard. The large man held the door open with one thick shoulder, eyeing me dubiously as he noticed my approach.

Before I could open my mouth to address the brute, another figure emerged. This figure, however, I instantly recognized.

Standing a full head shorter than myself, she wore a full, open-shouldered dress of not inconsiderable quality. Her golden hair was pulled back from her oval face and draped thickly down one shoulder. Her bright eyes, tinged with gold, widened when they noticed me. Her full lips parted in stunned breathlessness, emphasizing the small birthmark at one corner.

It would be most unjust to not say this woman was more than beautiful.

I'm unsure how long we both stood there, staring agape at one another, but before I could manage a single word, she whispered, "Ash?"

Understand, no one calls me Ash. In the world I have immersed myself in, very few even call me Asher, save a handful of closer acquaintances. Blinking back my surprise and regaining my composure, I nodded in customary respect.

"Lady Kaylock."

Lady Victoria Kaylock was a well-known figure in high-society London, and indeed her reputation was beginning to spread across the empire. She grew up in affluence, her father being the Honorable Lord Kaylock of Valen Hall, and had begun to rise in operatic circles, not chiefly due to her beauty but rather for her versatile singing range.

Lady Kaylock and I used to play together as children, although we were parted over unfavorable circumstances. I had not seen her in some years.

Her eyebrows knitted together, as if confused and frustrated in the same instant; then her face went void of expression. The flash of irritability likely stemmed from my using her formal title and not her first name. It was not customary nor honorable for someone of lower status, such as myself, to address a proper lady in such a fashion, even if we used to be childhood friends.

"Mr. Grey," Lady Kaylock began, readdressing me, "it has been too long since we last saw one another. How are you faring?"

"Well enough. I have no complaints," I replied, attempting to keep my tone even and detached. "What brings a lady of your status to a musty old corner like this one?"

Lady Kaylock lifted one hand to reveal that she was clutching a book. I had not even noticed it.

"Mr. Usher orders special books upon request and makes allowances for my tastes and schedule. I have been waiting for this copy of *Pride and Prejudice* by Ms. Austen for some time. First print."

"Yes, you have risen to quite a status, I hear. Congratulations."

A tinge of pink filled Lady Kaylock's cheeks, and she fumbled with her new book. "Thank you, Mr. Grey. But what about you? What occupies your time these days?"

"Consulting work, mostly," I answered nonchalantly. "I suppose I like to help where I'm needed."

A puzzling expression passed over the lady's face. Then, before either of us could continue, we were interrupted by a soft baritone.

"Lady, if I may, we must part. You are due at the London Opera House. Mr. Higgins is expecting your presence," the large bodyguard said expressionlessly.

Lady Kaylock glanced at the man.

"You're right, Gerard. We are behind, and Mr. Higgins does not appreciate tardiness," she said, sounding disappointed.

To our left, a private carriage rumbled to a halt only a few paces away, and Gerard stepped over to open the door. I watched in silence as the lady stepped up in her carriage with her bodyguard's assistance and then, sweeping her golden hair from one shoulder to the other, looked back in my direction.

"Mr. Grey."

"Yes, Lady."

"It wasn't entirely unpleasant seeing you again. Perhaps, if you are not busy, you would care to converse further? I typically attend Wendell's with several acquaintances for coffee. Perhaps you would care to join us? I would be quite interested in hearing more about your 'consulting' experiences. Are you familiar with Wendell's? In Trafalgar Square?"

"I am, Lady, although my consulting does keep me quite busy. I would hate to make you wait in vain. However, I will drop by, if I am able."

Again, her eyebrows knitted together, but only for an instant.

"Very well. Tomorrow night, then. Say, around nine o'clock? Do you have a pocket watch, Mr. Grey?" Her last question was clearly intended to prod me into reacting, reflecting her irritation at my detachment.

"I do," I replied. I pulled my old silver pocket watch from my breast pocket, and it popped open as I held it by the fob for her to see.

For the briefest of moments, that same mysterious expression flashed across Lady Kaylock's face; then, just as suddenly, it vanished.

"Very well, Mr. Grey. Tomorrow, perhaps. Gerard."

As Gerard joined Lady Kaylock, the dual horse team pulled swiftly, and the carriage rumbled away into the London crowds.

I was still holding out my open watch. I brought up my other hand to snap the latch shut when it dawned on me what was displayed inside. Opposite the clock face was a childhood picture of Victoria Kaylock.

Did she see it? Did she notice? I had to dismiss these distractions outright. Something was coming, something dark and dangerous. These thoughts were barriers that I must waste no time upon. I turned back to the Evening Star, stepped to the door, and grabbed the latch, only then noticing that I had been holding my breath.

To say the Evening Star bookstore is musty is not exactly accurate. In the dim light of its myriad yellow candles, the dark wood of the floors, walls, and shelving appear black. There is a gloom about the place that easily fits the proprietor's morose personality. A large, rounded counter sits to the left of the entrance, the wood glossy from countless elbows and books having passed over it. Behind the counter, against the wall, an ornate bookshelf encloses in glass the private collection of the Evening Star's master.

Atop the bookcase, on a makeshift roost built just for this purpose, perched a sizable raven. It turned its marble-like eyes toward me and cawed loudly, likely tossing some vulgarity at my person in his bird language. It ruffled black, pearlescent feathers in my direction.

"Nevermore, enough of your caterwauling! I can't concentrate when you go on like that! You know that!" snapped a voice to my right from amongst the rows of literature and documents.

"I don't think he likes me," I answered. "I don't think he ever has."

I heard a sudden shuffle, and a hunched form materialized from the gloom. Shambling up to the rounded counter with books under his arm was an old man far into his eighties. He had an large, bulbous head with wisps of white hair at the sides and a strangely pronounced brow that sat low and heavy over eyes, denoting a hint of melancholy. He arched one hairless brow in my direction.

"Bah, Nevermore doesn't much like anybody. He and I have that much in common," the old man croaked.

I smirked. "Edgar."

The old man crinkled his nose at me, more from annoyance than anger. "You know that's not my name anymore. It's Mr. Eugene Usher now, thank you very much."

"I know, I know. Usher. Yes, very discreet, Edgar. Don't you think somebody will catch on eventually? You named your raven Nevermore, for glory's sake."

Edgar waved his gnarled hand dismissively.

"Like whom? I could never resist an air of drama. Besides, no one would ever think to look for an American thought dead these past forty years in a bookstore in London. Moreover, the elderly are largely ignored en masse, anyway."

I shook my head, unable to hide my fondness for the old man.

Over forty years ago, Edgar had been a famous writer and poet in the Americas and was thought to have died suddenly of illness. Instead, the old man—tired and world weary—had laid down his old life of notoriety. Now he lived immersed in his research of all things arcane and occultic.

"What are you doing here, Grey?" Edgar asked absently as he set his books under the counter.

"What can you tell me about the Pale King?" I inquired bluntly.

The old man raised his creased face from behind the counter, the same brow arching quizzically.

"Eh? Pale King? Hmm. Seems I know that name from somewhere," he mumbled, turning his back to me to fidget with the locked glass bookcase behind him. He pulled out a small key from a chain around his neck to unlock the latch. "You on another case?" he asked.

"Just a bad feeling. There was a particularly difficult and unusual exorcism last night. The Pale King was mentioned."

Edgar swung the glass doors open wide and tugged one dusty tome from its depths. He dropped it heavily upon the counter.

"Heh. Aren't all exorcisms by definition unusual?"

I shook my head. "I was attacked by an Apepi demon taking passage in a gentleman. It was masquerading as an imp-level demon of fear. It attacked me outright, Edgar. It said it was an emissary of this Pale King."

Edgar's eyes widened. "Apepi? When was the last time anyone saw one of those?"

I shook my head but said nothing. The old bookstore owner turned a few pages in his antique book, then stopped on one entry.

"Here," he began, pointing to the page. "The Pale King. The Pale King is another name for Samhain, the demonic strongman of Scotland, dating back to the seventh century AD. It was said that the demon king used to walk the earth until he was banished."

I pulled out my journal and with a quill and ink from the counter took notation. My old leather journal contains insights into hundreds of cases—a resource I'm sure would be coveted by those of a darker alignment.

"Does it say *how* he was banished?" I asked.

Edgar shook his head. "No. But apparently the actual armor of the fiend was bound to him, then split apart and hidden. Heh, this seems a bit inconceivable, even for you."

I kept writing. "Does it say anything else?"

"Meh. Just that several cults have attempted to locate and gather the armor components to enact a ritual to bring back the demon to this plane."

I raised my head from my journal. "A ritual?"

"Yes, it binds a human victim to the armor, causing the dupe to become possessed by Samhain. Beh! That's pleasant."

I was appalled.

"*Forceful* demonization," I muttered. Swallowing to regain myself, I asked, "And I'm assuming the designated time of this ritual is on All Hallows' Eve?"

Edgar nodded. "At midnight."

I added my last notations to my journal, then slipped it beneath my overcoat.

This news was troubling. Few demonic creatures are known to be truthful, but it wasn't what that Apepi demon said that perplexed me—it was how it had been said. The demon was *boasting* as if what it threatened had already begun to unfold. That in itself left my heart unsettled.

Slapping my hand on the counter to snap myself from my brooding, I turned to the door.

"Thank you, Edgar."

The old man sighed. "I told you not to call me that," he grumbled, then added sarcastically, "Did you have any *more* questions, Mr. Grey?"

I opened the front door but stopped in the open portal.

"Yes. When did you start ordering books for Lady Kaylock?"

Edgar crossed his arms. "For a few months now. What's it to you, Grey? Don't tell me a pretty woman distracts you?"

"You are a miserable old man," I muttered, leaving the Evening Star.

I swore I heard guffawing as the door shut behind me, but whether it came from Edgar or his raven, I couldn't be sure.

CHAPTER 4

The Past and the Prophecy

Victoria Kaylock grew up on the Valen Hall estate in the Essex countryside, east of London. The estate, looked over by Lord and Lady Kaylock, comprised a sprawling manor house with open belts of well-maintained grasses and an elaborate hedge maze in the rear of the property.

Beyond the hedge maze was a wood that served as a marker for the boundary of the Valen Hall estate and the beginnings of the neighboring property.

The neighbors were lowborn—a coal miner and his family. They worked hard in the shadow of the high-living nobility. The husband labored in the mines and did carpentry for the Kaylocks on the side, while his wife was a relatively gifted grower of flowers, as well as an arranger of bouquets.

This is where my brother and I were raised until young adulthood. I do not often share my early years, as those times exist now only as echoes of a life far brighter and more innocent than the one in which I now live. My relationship with my brother is complicated at best, especially after the passing of both of our parents some years earlier.

My connection with Victoria, however, was one of simplicity in those days. We grew up as playmates, and although I was Victoria's senior by several years, we connected almost immediately. She didn't see a rough-and-tumble miner's son—simply a young boy attempting to find his place in the world just as much as she. The pair of us would meet and play secretly along our property border, hiding and seeking within the hedge maze.

Victoria was always beautiful, even as a child, although she enjoyed a boisterous and adventuresome spirit unusual for a child of English nobility. Over time, it became known that the Kaylocks' daughter had adopted the local boy as a playmate, which—as should come as no surprise—was met with mixed reactions. Lord Kaylock allowed the two of us to continue seeing each other, albeit with an air of caution. But Lady Kaylock became my enemy immediately, detesting her daughter's decision to soil her hands in association with me; however, she never strictly forbade our friendship in deference to Lord Kaylock.

Victoria and I became inseparable, and we spoke of many things, never keeping anything from one another.

But one autumn night, I was suddenly roused from sleep by my furious father demanding that I immediately awake and dress. Stepping into the entryway of our small home, I was shocked to find Lord and Lady Kaylock, with a sobbing Victoria in tow, standing before me.

Lady Kaylock was furious, accusing me of stealing her heirloom broach necklace, stating I had only befriended their precious daughter to purloin whatever I could nab. Lord Kaylock demanded I return the necklace, and my own family defended me, stating I had not the character to perform such an act.

I will always remember Victoria's face. The fear and uncertainty in her eyes. Oh, I attempted to defend my honor and contended that I had not, nor would ever, do such a thing, but I knew even then that it was in vain.

Lady Kaylock wanted me removed from her daughter's life, and she had discovered the perfect way to achieve just that.

Lord Kaylock threatened to involve the constabulary and have me jailed. When my father argued, Lord Kaylock announced he would end all employment for my parents, cutting off my family's income and ruining them. Seeing only one option, I fled the house that night, determining then and there to never return.

Looking back, I'm sure there were wiser decisions I could've made, but I was young and afraid and deeply troubled by the hardship my family was enduring because of me, whether I was innocent or not.

Needless to say, I never saw Victoria, or her family, again.

I sat lost in thought as the coach took me back to my tenement on Knight Street. The silver pocket watch lay open in my lap. Victoria had gifted it to me several months before my leaving Essex, but I' never had the heart to dispose of it.

I had naturally kept a finger on Victoria over the years. Several years after my departure, Lady Kaylock left Valen Hall and had made no contact since, causing gossip within the empire amidst the mention of some scandal. Not long after, and to add further scandal, Victoria began to sing within operatic circles, launching her meteoric rise in an unusual mix of fame and notoriety. Whether she took up this role in her interests or to restore the Kaylocks' reputation is unclear.

I could not deny that seeing Victoria again had thrown off my equilibrium. Exiting the hansom outside my home, I physically shook myself to dissolve the cobwebs and clear my head. Snapping the silver pocket watch shut, I shoved it back inside my breast pocket, paid for the cab, and stepped inside my flat.

I was upset with myself. There were far too many pressing matters at hand for me to indulge in fancies and distractions.

After visiting Edgar and finding out more about Samhain, the Pale King, I had spent the better portion of the afternoon allowing my hansom to take me on a tour of the city as I pondered all that had occurred in the last twelve hours. The day had slipped away, and night descended as I shut my tenement door behind me.

My flat was a modest place, a three-floor residence just over Waterloo Bridge in Southwark. The ground floor was strictly utilitarian, with kitchen and bath, while the second floor housed the guest bedroom as well as my own. The third floor was my study and also served as a passable library with a hearth at one end and a large, ocular-shaped window at the other that provided a not-unimpressive view of London.

Removing my overcoat, I ascended the stair to my room, where I tossed the coat onto my bed. I then ascended the remaining stairs in semidarkness to reach my study door.

Over the years, I've had my fair share of unwanted guests, intrusions, and surprise arrivals. So it did not completely startle me when I noticed candlelight emanating from beneath my door, as well as the gentle scuff of movement from within.

Clenching my fists, I prepared myself for who or what might be lying in wait within. My muscles tensed. I widened my stance and entered a crouch. I was sure that if there were multiple assailants, I could take on two, or perhaps three, with relative swiftness.

I took a deep breath and then stopped.

Lilacs. I smelled lilacs.

With the aroma came the immediate realization of who awaited me in my study. My tension eased, and I lowered my guard, but only slightly, permitting my muscles to relax but my mind to stay wary. I turned the door latch, pushed the door, and allowed it to swing open on its own.

Dim light washed over me from a single lit candle on the small, round table at the center of the room.

I casually stepped into my study and at once spotted a black figure reclined in my high-back chair by the hearth. Easing the door shut behind me, I moved to sit in the second chair that sat parallel to the first.

The dark figure was hooded with a long, black wrap that enclosed and hid the wearer's form. Their shifting ever so slightly produced a jingling sound, of bells or thin chains. The lower part of the figure's black wrap slid aside to reveal a woman's bare knee and calf as the scent of lilacs filled the room.

"Sabina," I said flatly.

The figure turned its hooded head to reveal the features of an exotically stunning woman.

"Asher," the woman replied with a thick Romany accent. "You look unwell. Are you not sleeping?"

"It's been an . . . involving few days. Why are you here, Sabina?" I asked, genuinely curious.

The woman tilted her head. Black curls spilled down her face, covering one eye.

How I met Sabina is a long story, originating back when I died but returned. That is irrelevant for now. What is relevant is that Sabina is enigmatic, unpredictable, and secretive. I have never been sure if I amuse or disgust her. She is a Gypsy prophetess with a knack for revealing facts that later come to pass.

"Why do I visit the infamous Asher Grey? Perhaps it is something I have heard in the Unseen World. Something about *you*." Her accent was thick, as always, and her habitual way of responding to my questions with questions sent an almost instant jolt of exasperation through my body. It was late, and it had been a full day. I was weary in mind and body.

"Is that why you traveled to my home this evening from Gypsy Hill? Because the Almighty mentioned my name?" I asked with more cynicism than I intended.

Sabina shifted her weight to lean on the chair arm closest to me. I could just make out her dusky eyes in the low light of the study.

"Sarcasm does not befit you, Asher Grey," she answered huskily, always saying my full name. "And your irreverence before the Power of Eternity is not necessarily wise. You are on another case, yes?"

I took a slow breath to ease my growing anxieties. She was right: it was dishonorable to spew negativity toward Heaven, no matter the mood I was in. Something brought Sabina all the way here from Norwood's Gypsy camp in South London. I must be patient.

"Yes, in a way. I have no client at the moment, but I am exploring a potential threat of a more diabolical nature that has reared its head of late."

Sabina rose from her seat and moved toward the solitary candle at the room's center. I stood as well and followed. The gypsy slowly moved around the table, across from me, gliding her fingers across its surface.

"Forces are stirring," Sabina whispered, "both celestial and infernal. Something of insidious and dark intent is coming."

She turned toward me then, keeping the candle between us. The light of it revealed an alluring, olive-skinned woman dressed in a sarong of black linens. The way it was wrapped around Sabina's form revealed the bare flesh of her torso and legs, which was utterly scandalous by societal standards. For some reason, however, I did not believe that concept occurred to or concerned the Gypsy in the slightest.

"What am I contending with here?" I asked, also in a whisper.

"The horror which is attempting to enter this world is an abomination of malevolence. It is the very spirit of balefire, and longs to incinerate and consume the world," Sabina answered, her eyes off focus as if looking over a great distance.

"Is there a method by which it can be impeded from making an entrance into this plane?" I asked.

Sabina again tilted her head to one side, causing another long lock of curly black hair to fall loosely from her hood. Her eyes stared straight ahead, straight through me. She nodded slowly.

"There is a way. The ritual must be thwarted before its completion—"

"On All Hallows' Eve," I mumbled.

Sabina continued, with caution in her tone, "It is not the hellish fiend that is the immediate threat, Asher Grey, but the man by which the fiend is maneuvering to bring about its twisted birth. This man—*he* is whom you must be steeled against. He and his devotees."

Hmm, I thought. *Devotees*. Sabina must have been alluding to one of the various cults Edgar had read about, and this singular individual was their overseer or high priest. I would need to discover what group, where they were gathering, and who this shadowy leader might be. Someone somewhere had to have seen or heard of a group rallying for a dark purpose on All Hallows' Eve.

One individual came to mind who almost certainly knew something. Unfortunately, we did not have much of a rapport. *Well, he will just have to suffer my company nevertheless*, I decided. I needed answers.

Sabine spoke again, breaking into my thoughts. "Be mindful—wary—of his fortune teller."

"Fortune teller?"

"You will know her by the snakes," Sabine said blankly.

"What?"

Sabine has the knack for being enigmatic, but that is to be expected. Prophetic messages from the Highest are often random, disjointed, and discursive. How could they be anything else? The Unseen World does not function as ours does, and I have come to understand over multiple encounters, with Sabina and others like her, that prophecy is not an exact science.

I pulled out my old leather journal and used a nearby stick of charcoal to scribble the Gypsy's strange utterings. There was more to this business with the Pale King than I originally perceived back at Bedlam with Mr. George Brand. Maybe much more.

"A cult leader and a fortune teller," I repeated. "Anything else?"

Sabina's eyes dropped slowly to the lit candle on the table between us. She arched one black eyebrow.

"Lancashire," she said, thickly pronouncing the English name in her Romany accent.

"Lancashire?"

"When your heart fails, look to Lancashire," she said slowly, as if unsure of her own words.

This seemed even more peculiar than normal, and not a little foreboding. I decided to trust my discernment and take note of this as well. Putting away my journal, I glanced back at Sabina. The shrouded Gypsy had already turned from the candle and moved to the door. A recipient of prophetic utterances does not need a recovery period as mediums or diviners do. This is because prophets need only yield to a Higher Power, whereas others always have to give a part of themselves.

Having delivered the messages she had come to confer, Sabina glided from the study and down the stairs. I said nothing and merely followed. The Gypsy was not one for small talk or unnecessary gestures.

When Sabina reached the front door of my tenement, however, she abruptly paused and turned back to face me. Looking unblinkingly into my eyes, she said, "Asher Grey, you have walked a lonely road all of your life, and been witness to visitations, miracles, and portents. When we found you those years ago, freshly returned from the Unseen World, there was a separateness to you, and because of this, you have had to construct a wall around your heart to protect yourself. But now, Asher Grey," she said with a faintly bemused smile, "it is good to see you like this."

"Like what?" I asked.

Sabina turned her back to me and opened the door. The night air brought the fragrance of lilacs once again to my nostrils.

"Vulnerable," the gypsy said, and she stepped out into the night and vanished.

As always, Sabina did not bother to shut the door behind her. As I descended the stairs to do so myself, my mind attempted to grasp the meaning of the Gypsy's parting words.

Vulnerable? I am somehow vulnerable?

I searched my own heart for what was lacking that was not before. Growing irritated, I dismissed the Gypsy's last assumption and retired to bed, unwilling to give it another thought.

Only later would I realize what a mistake that was.

CHAPTER 5

Consultation with the Doctor

LONDON

October 29

There are, regrettably, many burrows and quarters within Greater London that have fallen into disrepair, and many more that exist almost entirely in squalor. As a result, rising author Charles Dickens once penned, "many thousands are in want of common necessaries; hundreds of thousands are in want of common comforts." It would be fabrication to claim that the destitution within the realm does not vex me greatly. It always has.

One might be discomfited for various obvious and humane points, from the gangs of orphans and urchins huddled in the night for warmth to the near starvation of many a family. As prosperous and immense as the British Empire is, and as I am one of those citizens who grew up without a silver spoon in my mouth, that does not hold well with me.

Moreover, another major concern connected with the vast slums of London uniquely affects my professions: supernatural malevolence always seems to congregate in these crestfallen regions. Whatever is wicked, whatever is twisted—if anything is born in darkness, it can be found in the slums.

But I digress.

It was in one of these areas of dilapidation that I found myself the next day. At the east end of London is Whitechapel. I strode amongst the ruffians, street peddlers, prostitutes, urchins, and drunkards in search of the personage whom Sabina's prophetic warnings made me recall.

This "gentleman"—and I use the term loosely, as his reputation is far from commendable—was said to have settled here to conduct bizarre and mystical experimentation where he would not be bothered by those of a more moral bent—or the constabulary, for that matter. He was Austrian and reputed to be an architect, although those immersed in the unearthly and peculiar declared him to be a clairvoyant and alchemist.

Now, I do not conduct myself in my tasks as an exorcist in alliance with anything of a fiendish nature. This happens to be a point that I take *very* seriously, as I have been witness to far too much to deny that there is an Almighty, and I am under his employ. This is also a matter of personal pride to me, much to the chagrin of many who have offered in the past to collaborate.

With that distinctly stated, I wish to make it clear that I was not seeking out this Austrian in the hopes of forming a partnership; I sought answers in the same manner as a Scotland Yard inspector questions a suspect. The Austrian's name was Rudolf Steiner, and over the last several hours, I had laboriously dropped his name to well-nigh every prostitute, barroom proprietor, seedy landlord, and street rat I came across.

Air in this area of London is not what one could with integrity even call air—more a miasma of odors, thick with the black smog of coal that quite literally burns the nostrils and lungs with any deep inhale. Around me flowed an ocean of wicked acts and woebegone scenes no morally straight man should become accustomed to. I passed by a dozen naked boys bathing in a massive puddle in the street, then stepped aside as a toothless man pushing a wheelbarrow filled with what I assumed was excrement lumbered by, humming absently to himself.

Stopping to ask if several impoverished-looking elderly women had heard of the Austrian, I noticed a young, willowy girl several paces away whose ears perked up at Steiner's name.

Casually, I padded toward her, noticing quickly that she was a child of probably no more than ten—a match girl, by the look of her small wooden tray of wares. It was still midday, and even in the murky air of Whitechapel, I detected the far-too-premature lines of weariness on the girl's face, signs of a difficult life.

"Matches, governor?" the girl asked in a mousy tone. Her hair was coal black and matted with grease to her face.

"All right," I said. "I'll take a dozen off your hands." I reached into my pocket for what change I had.

"A *dozen*, sir?" the girl asked incredulously. "Why, thank you. Thank you, sir. That's two pennies, sir."

I reached out and put a full pound in the girl's dirty, outstretched hand, taking the matches in return. She looked down and, when she realized what I had given to her, adamantly exclaimed her gratitude.

"Oh! Thank you! Thank you, sir!"

"What's your name?" I asked.

The girl's expression faltered, and a look of wariness and unease filled her eyes.

"Christine," she all but whispered.

"Do not fear me, Christine," I said reassuringly. "I have no ill intentions. I simply wish to ask you a question. Earlier, when I inquired of those women over there about Mr. Rudolf Steiner, you seemed to recognize the name. You know him, don't you, Christine?"

The match girl's eyes widened slightly.

"Please, sir. I don't want no trouble," Christine pleaded. "The doctor, he has eyes everywhere. If he sees me telling someone about him . . ." She trailed off.

My discernment sent a chill down my back. As Christine glanced nervously about her, I became increasingly aware of hidden eyes upon us, eyes attached to minds who wished to do me harm. I did not get the impression that they were diabolical or infernal; rather, the malevolence was carnal and worldly: the intent of wicked men.

With a quick nod to the frightened match girl to signal to her that I understood her plight, I turned swiftly on my heel to divert attention and draw my potential assailants' maliciousness upon myself.

I darted down one narrow side street, ducking and dodging a spiderweb of clotheslines covered in assorted worn garments and underclothes. When I reached the far end, I ventured a look over my shoulder and espied at least one figure in pursuit of me, weaving through the hanging laundry as I had.

I lunged toward a constricting alley to my right, turning my body flat against one soiled brick wall to squeeze myself through to the other side. I heard boots scuffling on the gravel behind me but did not look back. I had to stay focused on attaining an advantage over my pursuers. It would only be a matter of moments before I had to defend myself and no longer had the luxury of fleeing.

Emerging from the confined passage, I found myself in a derelict stable, nearly stumbling headfirst into a mound of decaying straw. I rushed promptly toward the rear of the ramshackle structure, intent on discovering an exit or a place to hide until my trackers passed by.

It was with immediate disappointment that I observed nowhere to which I could flee, as the rear of the barn had collapsed some time ago, falling in upon itself. Behind me, I heard footsteps and voices of more than one aggressor as they discovered my narrow passage and entered in pursuit.

Now, I am not a stranger to violence. I have faced down my fair share of brigands, ruffians, and highwaymen in my career and even before that, during my years abroad, enlisted in Her Majesty's army in Crimea and Afghan. I do not possess a fear of or aversion to the use of brute strength. However, I much prefer using my wits and negotiation to fisticuffs any day.

Taking a deep breath, I stood straight and pushed my shoulders back. Then, turning about, I strolled casually back to where my pursuers waited.

I beheld five figures—all shabbily dressed, thick-shouldered ruffian types. I perceived immediately that they were hoods: hired muscle for someone with the pockets to keep them satisfied with coin or booze. One of the five stood out above the rest, as he wore the tall top hat of a gentleman, although it was torn and covered with grime, as was the rest of him.

"'Ello, look what we got 'ere, boys," he sneered in thick Cockney. "Looks like we got ourselves a lost sheep, eh?"

The other mugs leered and chuckled. Every last one revealed mouths full of rotting teeth. They began to move closer, several paces from me. I had to do something fast.

"Gentlemen," I said calmly, almost warmly, "perhaps one of you fine chaps would be kind enough to direct me to the nearest pub? See, I am parched and in desperate need of a constitutional. Say, perhaps I could purchase a round for you helpful gentlemen. What do you say to a fine beer with me?"

The group peered at each other, unsure of how to react. As confusion spread across their faces, I suspected that my plan was succeeding, until I glanced back at their leader in the top hat. A slow grin etched its way across his gaunt and grungy face, a grin filled with yellow teeth and cunning.

"Oh ho," he said, "but you ain't lookin' for a beer. You're 'ere 'cause you're looking for the doctor."

"I'm quite sure I don't have the slightest notion of what you're talking about. I'm simply looking to purchase—"

"We saw you! You've been askin' 'bout the doctor all over town, so you can drop the fop routine, eh?"

I shrugged and sighed. "Very well. You work for Rudolf Steiner, I presume, and he pays you to what? Run off any poor soul who wanders into the streets, foolish enough to look for him?"

Top Hat grinned even wider. "That's right. Like you."

"Fair enough. But what if Dr. Steiner *wants* to see me? Would that not alter your orders to waylay me?"

Top Hat sniffed and wiped his nose with the back of his hand.

"Oh, yeah, maybe. But I be knowin' for certain that the doctor don't want to be seein' *you* 'ere."

"Is that right?" I queried. "And how do you take such certainty in that? Perhaps he might find me to be a delight."

"'Ardly, I'd say. We know who ya are, Mr. Asher Grey, and we've been instructed to drop ya to the bottom of the Thames if we come across ya."

The mob began to move forward, the four brigands stepping around their top-hatted leader. The closest raised his hands to grab at me.

As I stated, I do not desire violence, but there's a time when it becomes necessary. When it does, one must not only overpower his opponents but outthink them as well.

I exploded into motion, lunging toward the closest thug. Caught off guard, he attempted to raise his hands to defend himself, but I caught him square in the nose. This resulted in a cry of surprise and pain as his nostrils erupted in blood. He staggered back, and his companion leaped at me from around his collapsing friend.

I ducked under the attacker's outstretched arms, tackling him in the midsection, and with a quick upward thrust sent him flipping over my shoulder to land on his back behind me.

Before I could prepare for the next assailant, though, the third rowdy punched me heavily across the cheek. I was half spun about but managed to keep my footing and raised an arm just in time to parry a second blow. Having successfully blocked the strike, I thrust my head forward, sending my forehead crashing into the man's chin. He tottered back unsteadily, so I promptly dropped him to the ground with a downward punch to the cheek.

All at once, I found my arms pinned to my body by a bear hug from behind; the man I had flipped had recovered. The fourth ruffian reached me and immediately took advantage of my helpless state by bludgeoning me hard in the ribs once, then twice.

Pain shot through my body, but survival cried out louder. I lifted my legs off the ground, bending my knees up to my chest, then kicked them out together, slamming both feet into the man's face. He went down in a heap.

The moment my feet landed on the ground, I launched my head backward with a crunch as my occipital collided with the nose of the man bear-hugging me. His hold loosened, and I broke free. I spun on him then and with one wide-swung uppercut laid the thug out flat on his back.

I stood motionless for a moment to ensure that the attackers could not attempt another assault. When I knew they were truly incapacitated, I straightened and turned squarely toward the man with the top hat, who had not made a move since his lackeys' scuffle began.

I tugged at my overcoat to compose myself and leveled a hard gaze at him.

"If you knew I was Asher Grey, then you should've known better," I said flatly.

Top Hat's grin had faltered, giving way to an expression of uncertainty. He attempted to settle himself and, donning his cocky grin once again, like a mask, took one step back.

I sniffed and raised my face in confidence.

"Maybe you should introduce me to this doctor now."

My discernment screamed to me like a fire bell as I followed the top hat–adorned brigand and his group of thugs. Each of them carried themselves a bit differently now. There was a palpable feeling of shame and defeat; their faces were downcast and their shoulders hunched. And there was something else: fear. Tangible and raw.

Perhaps it was because these men were about to face their taskmaster, but regardless, I braced myself.

Top Hat led the way through the back alleyways of Whitechapel, finally coming to a disused factory. We entered through a side door and walked across what had once been the work floor but was now an empty gravel expanse. As we approached the far brick wall, I noticed a patch of masonry had been knocked through, revealing a portal going down. I could just detect a series of rough, uneven steps fading into the murky blackness.

I kept my wits about me and my senses on watch, not just for the chaps around me but also on the darkening environs as we descended underground.

"The catacombs, is it?" I asked, eyeing the brick tunnels as Top Hat lit a lantern.

"Aye, yeah," he mumbled. "The doctor enjoys a bit of privacy, he does."

I had, over the years, ventured down into several different sections of London's underground, but never in this area of the city. The ancient catacombs beneath England's capital date back to Ancient Rome and span hundreds of miles in all directions.

After what seemed like an hour of navigating side passages and offshoot corridors, we reached a slight widening in our way that ended abruptly at a relatively new, thick, timber door.

Light leaked out from beneath, and the men around me paused when we neared.

"Wait 'ere," Top Hat said, setting the lantern down at my feet. He turned to face the door, straightened his sullied jacket with a deep breath, and gave one hard knock.

After a moment, a voice from within cried, "Enter!" Top Hat opened the door, then disappeared within, closing it behind him.

I affected nonchalance as I regarded the other four men. They demonstrated a noticeable aversion to the door, so I addressed them as a whole.

"So, what type of a man is this doctor?"

The lot of them glanced at one another uneasily. One managed to speak up after an audible gulp.

"We don't wanna speaks no ills o' the docta. No one goes 'gainst da likes o' 'im. 'E's . . . in possession of powers—unnatural powers. Don't be underestimatin' 'im."

"Powers?" My discernment flashed. There definitely was *something* here with the doctor.

Another of the thugs chimed in. "'E turned our old pal Dodga into, well, into somethin' unnatural, 'e did, when Dodga disobeyed 'im. Somethin' downright disturbin'."

I arched an eyebrow. "Turned him into something? Oh, come now."

"Now, you look 'ere!" a third goon interjected. "We ain't makin' this up! We seen it wit' our own eyes, we did! Dodga was all twisted and warped like . . . like one of them wee rag dolls after da dog's shaken it up a bit."

"You'll be seein' for yourself soon," the first man said. "Da doctor's got powers to change any manner o' beast. You . . . you been warned."

The timber door cracked open, interrupting the mob's bizarre counsel. Top Hat appeared from within, pale in the face.

"Da doctor will be seein' you now, Mr. Grey," he said with a flat, blank tone, as if reading from a cue card.

Cracking my neck to one side to ease the tension and settle my nerves, I advanced toward the top-hatted man and entered the adjoining room. I faintly recollect the door closing behind me, but I was utterly diverted in my attention by the room before me: a long, spacious chamber with a high, domed ceiling.

I advanced, pacing through a space equal parts library and laboratory. Tables lining either side were covered in beakers, files, and tubes filled with strangely colored liquids. Beyond these were shelves of books and parchments standing some five to eight heads higher than I was tall.

At the far end of the chamber stood a massive oak table some ten spans long. It was fully overlaid with parchments, diagrams, and various yellowed papers. Just to the right was an impressive operating table surrounded by benches and trays displaying all of the tools of the doctoral and medicinal trades. Disturbingly, though, a large and bloody tarp covered a shape lying on the medical table—something big.

"Well then," came a voice to my immediate left. "You must be the notorious Asher Grey."

I turned my attention toward the owner of the voice and spied a man of average height and build who seemed to be in his mid-twenties. He had the airs of a gentleman, with chestnut hair and a mustache oiled thickly in a peculiar fashion I had never seen before. The dark, bristly hair swept out and upward to such wide degrees that the mustache jutted out from the sides of his face several centimeters.

When he stepped closer opposite me across the huge oak table, I noticed he had donned the academic robe of a medical doctor or professor, and all manner of tools hung from a half dozen belts crisscrossing his body.

"I am Asher Grey," I replied, "and I can only assume I'm in the presence of the famous Dr. Steiner?"

Clicking his heels together and bowing slightly, the man answered, "I am Dr. Rudolph Steiner. It is evident to me that my men did not harm you. This is good. Leave us!" he commanded Top Hat behind me, who blanched and, quickly bowing, vanished from the room. I had the distinct impression that the doctor was not finished dealing with his hired muscle and that some severe penalty awaited them for not dealing with me as ordered.

I glanced back at Dr. Steiner, who was studying me like a child does an ape at Barnum's Circus.

"No, I'm quite all right. Not for a lack of trying on their part, however."

"Indeed," replied the doctor, his every word dripping with a thick Germanic accent. "Why have you come and disturbed me from my work, Mr. Grey?"

"Work, Dr. Steiner?"

"I am a researcher and devotee of many fields dealing with the boundaries of the scientific and metaphysical. I delve into those spheres that my contemporaries have labeled unnatural, Mr. Grey."

"I see. You are eccentric in their eyes, then?" I supposed.

"I'm *mad* in their eyes, Mr. Grey. Or dangerous. Either way, my critics merely cower in fear of what only I have the intrepidness to do."

I looked about the vast laboratory and sanctum. My discernment told me clearly that the interests of this man reeked of sorcery and the black arts. Although I was equipped with a few abilities of my own, I had to be cautious around this deranged but very intelligent man.

I decided to shift the subject to keep Dr. Steiner absorbed in his ego.

"In all your doubtlessly stalwart ventures, have you ever come across any cultic groups about London?"

"Feh!" he exclaimed dismissively with a wave of his hand. "There are more clubs, fraternities, and brotherhoods in this poor excuse for a city than there are gaslights. Most are far more directed toward hedonism, wealth, or their agendas to be considered anything more than social clubs. There is a . . . smattering, however, that could be regarded as committed to a cause."

"And what about one that's doctrinally devoted to something of a more infernal nature—say, the Pale King?"

There was an immediate reaction on the doctor's face; his detached, self-absorbed expression became one of intense focus. "What did you say?" he whispered.

"Samhain, the Pale King," I clarified.

Dr. Steiner looked down at his parchments on the table before him. "There is one group. I encountered their like but once, about a year ago. I was interested in locating several items of rare and mystical import. I happened upon a particular gentleman who claimed to be in the market for several rare artifacts. A suit of ancient armor, I think. In opening up a conversation with the man, a distinct feeling of precariousness came over me, and I developed an immediate impulse to part from his company."

"Do you remember this gentleman's name?" I inquired.

"No," Steiner replied. "I did not wish to be any more intimate with the man—he or his odd, fortune-telling consort."

"What?" I asked, caught off guard.

"Yes, he had in his company a strange woman, very exotic. White hair with tattoos. She never left his side but whispered constantly into his ear. It made me unsettled."

"Snakes?"

"Hmm?"

"Those tattoos. Were they snakes, by chance?"

"Why, yes," he said with suspicion. His eyes narrowed. "Yes, they *were*."

"Dr. Steiner, what is the name of their group? Where can I find them? You know, don't you?"

The Austrian gripped the table and leaned forward to glare intensely into my eyes, his own revealing growing worry and annoyance.

"What are you involved in, Grey? What have you brought to my door?" he demanded.

I raised my hands. "Nothing, Dr. Steiner. I'm only looking into an issue that may be something or nothing. I will say that if this issue *does* prove to be something, hiding down in these catacombs will no longer keep you unnoticed. And no one will be safe."

"And I am to assume that if this issue does indeed progress into something, that *you*, Mr. Grey, plan on thwarting it?" the doctor asked, sounding dubious.

"I will," I answered flatly.

Steiner sighed and took several steps down the length of the table and past me. He kept his back to me, and I believed our conversation had come to a close. I prepared to leave disappointed.

Until, shockingly, he spoke.

"The Thirteenth Pentacle. That was the name of his ... group. The Thirteenth Pentacle. They frequent Vauxhall Gardens, just outside Chelsea, over the Vauxhall Bridge. He invited me there once to join them, this distressing man. I declined, of course, excused myself, and hastily escaped his company."

"I see," I said, not a little surprised at the sudden change in the doctor's behavior, from threatening to somewhat yielding. This man with the fortune teller the doctor spoke of must have unnerved the Austrian far more deeply than he wanted to portray.

"When do they have their coming together?"

"When else? At the midnight hour, of course," he replied derisively.

I nodded. "Of course."

I hastily scribbled down the information Dr. Steiner had given me: THE THIRTEENTH PENTACLE, VAUXHALL GARDENS, MIDNIGHT. My mind raced to plan, strategizing how to infiltrate this cult, discover if they were, in fact, a threat, and put an end to any deviousness. The biggest and growing concern was that there might be an attempt to bring this Pale King into this plane. I had to discover if this was possible.

This was about to be a long and taxing evening.

I put away my journal and turned to depart. "Thank you for your assistance, Dr. Steiner. I will be sure to put this information to good use that will benefit all of us."

"Just do me this one service, Mr. Grey," he replied. "Leave this place and never return. If you do, I will not be as ... cordial as I have been tonight."

CHAPTER 6

Coffee with an Old Friend

After navigating the labyrinth of catacombs and safely returning to the streets of London, I caught a hansom with haste and traveled back to the warmth and safety of my flat on Knight's Street.

It had been an exhausting two days, and I was irritated by the direction in which this investigation appeared to be heading. The possibility of a demonic ritual, even the slightest possibility, would not make any man excited, let alone at peace.

I collapsed into one of the high-back chairs in my study and slipped into unconsciousness.

My mind drifted in a sea of imagery both disturbing and macabre: Hooded cult members with no faces danced about pyres of green flames alongside imps and snakes. At one point, Edgar was there, reading a book, oblivious to the horrific revelry all about him. I spied Sabina there, too, making some gesture to me, which I could not interpret.

When I awoke, I realized the day had fled, and I slumped in my chair, only a little more rested than before.

Making my way to the bath, I cleaned myself up, which did bring refreshment. Upon inspection in my mirror, I noticed that the water had brought an end to the bags of weariness I had carried beneath my eyes since midday. I put on fresh clothes and descended to the kitchen, where I prepared for myself several eggs and leftover pork loin I had enjoyed earlier that week.

It is remarkable what a meal, some rest, and a bath can do for the constitution. I felt like a new man.

Grabbing my overcoat, I departed my tenement, hailed a coach, and rode off into the night.

As the hansom trundled through the sights and sounds of London by night, my mind pored over all that I had uncovered about this affair and pondered what I was to do about it. Though wary of Steiner's interests and motivations, I had no doubt that this fanatical cult, the Thirteenth Pentacle, was indeed active in London as he claimed. Also, they seemed to be not only recruiting but also searching for the collection of Samhain armor components in time to enact their dark ritual and bring the Pale King into this world by All Hallows' Eve, just three nights hence.

Who was this front man that led them? Something deep down in my gut, whether instinct or discernment, gave me a very uneasy feeling regarding this gentleman—and not only him but the fortune teller who appeared to be aiding him. I sensed the demonic all over them both, and when I get that impression, I trust it.

I was also keenly aware that I had no real client in this investigation, which is not a precondition for me to do my work. But one fact *was* essential: no clients means no pay. Battling the demonic and unnatural does not bring much income as is. Although I have been brought back from death before, I certainly am not immortal by any means and regrettably still require food in my belly. Taking a case with no monetary benefit would not help matters.

But this is a moral predicament that I have often grappled with, and even when there appeared to be no financial benefit, the Almighty has always seen fit to bring about just what was needed to make ends meet.

I do work for Him, after all. And besides, who else would do it?

In the midst of these long roads of thought, I was brought back to the present circumstances by the coachman of my hansom.

"'Ey, mista! Ya gonna get out of me cab? Dis is where ya said to be goin'! Wendell's, right off Trafalgar Square!"

Looking about, I realized that in my enthrallment with the case, I had evidently taken a cab to Wendell's to dine with Victoria's company. I could not explain what had inspired me to come, especially since I had made up my mind to dismiss her invitation entirely.

Yet here I stood, and as I paid the coachman, disembarked the cab, and ascended the white marble stairs of the establishment, I felt a certain disquiet combined with an exhilaration that I had not experienced before—nor could I make sense of it.

This dining establishment is typically populated by the elite, nobility, and royalty of Her Majesty's empire, so I was quickly identified as being out of place amidst such prominence. All within were adorned in formal dining attire, tuxedos, and dressing gowns, while I boasted the worn gray overcoat that I always wore, with only a vest and shirt beneath.

"Might I help you, sir?" a voice asked from my left.

It belonged to an older man with oiled white chops who possessed the appearance of the maître d' of Wendell's. The look of dubiousness and irritation on his brow told me that I was not wanted there.

"Yes. I'm here to meet Lady Kaylock. Is her party here?"

The maître d' raised his eyebrows.

"Ermm . . . *you*, sir?"

"That's right. Where is she seated?"

"Ehh, just over there, near the window, sir." He pointed. "May I take your overcoat, sir?"

"No, thank you," I replied and headed in the direction the old elitist specified.

As I weaved through the busy establishment, I was met with leers from members of the gentry. It did not take long to locate the table I was searching for. Up against one thickly draped, arched window was a head of golden-blond hair I recognized immediately as belonging to Lady Victoria Kaylock.

One could easily state that Lady Kaylock is one of the most genuinely lovely women in London, if not the world. She is known not only for her noble upbringing and her enchanting singing voice but also her exquisite features. She took a small sip of what I presumed was coffee, then sat down the cup as a woman seated with her laughed at something that only she found hilarious.

I took a deep breath to brace my nerves and approached the table. But before I could speak, a huge shape surged forward from near the window to my left and came to stand directly between the table and myself.

"Gerard," I sighed, looking up into the block-shaped face of Victoria's bodyguard.

The big man only grunted in reply, but before any words could be exchanged, a far gentler voice emerged from behind him.

"Ash—*Mr*. Grey. You decided to join us. That will be all, Gerard. Mr. Grey was invited."

Gerard turned to look over his shoulder, revealing Lady Kaylock eyeing the both of us with expectancy. The thick bodyguard lumbered back to his position by the window, but not without giving me one last glance that suggested bodily harm if I intended to cross any lines with his employer.

I moved to an empty chair to Victoria's left and across from her friend, and sat heavily.

Lady Kaylock raised her eyebrows. "I am surprised you managed to join us. Not too busy, I see."

There was a taunt in her voice—an edge of irritability. When we were children, she always had a knack for provoking a response in me. But that was then, and we were not children anymore.

"I found some time not allocated to anything. Besides, I was in the vicinity. My lady," I lied.

Lady Kaylock knitted her eyebrows together for a brief moment, then gestured to the woman next to her. "This is Lady Roxanne Pemberton of Kent. Lady Pemberton, this is Mr. Asher Grey."

"Madam," I said with a nod.

Lady Pemberton appeared to be a few years Lady Kaylock's elder, with wavy red locks and green eyes. She could be said to be pretty, but with a slight worldliness to her bearing despite a noble pedigree.

Her eyes widened with a look of unmistakable surprise and pleasure.

"Mr. Grey!" she exclaimed, a grin building. "You're not Mr. Asher Grey that has had his hands in all manner of ghosts, spirits, and supernatural oddities? You are! How wonderful!"

Lady Pemberton did not allow me to respond but continued her enthusiastic rant while Victoria sat stunned, looking back and forth between her friend and me. An expression of bewilderment grew upon her face.

"Oh, Victoria," Lady Pemberton continued, "you never told me you knew Asher Grey! Why, my auntie told me all about him! You deal in hauntings, curses, and the like! My auntie said you removed a demon from the church in Buckingham, and then set fire to the church afterward! Oh, Victoria, this man is so delightfully interesting!"

Lady Kaylock turned her surprised eyes to me, apparently speechless.

"It wasn't so much a demon," I began, attempting to bring the conversation under control, "as it was a cursed item. And I didn't burn down the church. I merely burned some furniture connected to the curse to be sure the church was cleansed."

Lady Pemberton clapped her hands in glee. Lady Kaylock did not look amused.

"I am confused. You told me you were a *consultant*," she said.

"I am," I answered.

"Consulting mystic and exorcist, Victoria," interrupted Lady Pemberton.

"Surely not!" Victoria exclaimed.

I shook my head. "No, no. I am not a mystic. But yes, I am someone who has performed an occasional exorcism."

Lady Kaylock's eyes widened as if she were being addressed by a madman. She radiated a definite air of displeasure at not already knowing these facts and discomfort in knowing she now did. I could tell she did not know what to make of all this.

My mouth grew dry, either from the long day or the unpretentious conversation I had found myself in. I flagged a waiter and asked for coffee. Thankfully, it arrived quickly.

"I heard you can read minds. Is that true?" asked Lady Pemberton.

I took a sip of coffee to buy time to gather my patience. I began to believe that coming here had been a mistake.

"No, that's not true," I answered, "although I do get feelings from time to time."

I glanced at Victoria. I remembered that searching and perturbed look from our childhood. It did not usually mean anything good.

"Roxanne," Victoria said calmly to her friend, "would you be so kind as to find the maître d' and request my shawl? I seem to have taken a chill in this drafty old building."

Lady Pemberton threw up her hands in mock resignation but retained her wide eyes and smirk. "Now, Victoria, I *did* tell you not to check it in upon our arrival, and now here you are, about to catch your death of cold."

After the boisterous redhead rose from the table, Victoria turned her penetrating attention upon me. I braced for an outpouring of irritation and wrath.

"So, is there anything you would like to tell me, or are you pleased with accepting my invitation this evening only to give your attention to Lady Pemberton and her banter?"

Victoria was irritated that her friend knew far more about my life than she did and not a little displeased that I was locked in dialogue with Lady Pemberton. *Is that jealousy I detect? Could Victoria be envious after all this time?* I wondered.

From the look of her flushed cheeks and protruding bottom lip, I had taken too long to respond. Before I could open my mouth, Victoria demanded, "Are you going to tell me, or not?"

I cleared my throat. "Tell you . . . ?"

"Oh, stop it! You know exactly what I'm asking you."

"Look, Lady Kaylo—"

"*Stop* calling me that, Ash! My name is *Victoria*! We go too far back for that nonsense! What happened to you? Where did you go? What is all this piffle Roxanne is saying about you?"

This was the Victoria I remembered from years past: boisterous, no-nonsense, and aggressively direct. The fact that she immediately dismissed all formalities and demanded the use of first names lowered my inhibitions in responding. At this moment, she was no longer Lady Kaylock of Valen Hall. She was Victoria, the girl-turned-woman of my youth.

I wrapped both hands around my coffee cup and looked into the depths of the black steaming liquid within. "When I told you yesterday that I was a consultant, that was true. I am employed by anyone seeking understanding, insight, or freedom from issues or circumstances of a more . . . otherworldly nature. Sometimes, yes, the circumstances might involve elements of a more gruesome or vile bent. People hire me to remove those elements."

Victoria listened wide eyed. I had seen that same expression when I was accused of stealing Lady Kaylock's broach. It was an expression of disbelief.

"So, demons, ghosts, and the like?" she asked.

I nodded. "And witches, curses, or other more sinister situations that occasionally vex humanity."

I noticed Victoria's hands were clutching a cloth napkin absently but tightly as she looked down into her lap.

"Is this why you ran away?" she whispered.

Almost instantly, ire surged from my belly—anger from the old wounds of the past.

"What else could I do? It was a radical course, I admit, but what alternative did I have? Your parents, Lord and Lady Kaylock, were threatening not only to throw me into prison but also to destroy my family, making them destitute. I never stole that broach of your mother's, but no one believed me, so I ran."

Looking up quickly, Victoria's face turned red. "What do you mean, 'no one'?"

"I saw your face, saw the look of doubt in your eyes while you wept, clutching your father!" I exclaimed.

"What?" Victoria blurted. "I thought you knew me better than that!"

What is this? I thought. *Am I understanding this correctly? Did Victoria trust that I did not steal the broach?*

My mind was immediately flooded with overwhelming feelings of shame and embarrassment at the ramifications of what had occurred. I sighed and took a sip of my coffee so as not to meet Victoria's hurt gaze.

"That was all a long time ago," I muttered in an attempt to change the topic. "I'm not the same person anymore—the boy that I was. It doesn't matter now."

Victoria gasped; then quietly, intensely, she said, "What do you mean 'It does not matter'? *Yes*, it *does*."

I lifted my eyes to hers and found tears. She was in as much anguish over her past as I was at mine. *Can it be that the frustration and offense we have both been harboring all these years is founded upon a misunderstanding or misinterpretation of the facts?*

Before I could open my mouth to respond, Lady Roxanne Pemberton blustered up to the table, forcefully wrapping Victoria in the shawl she had requested.

"Would you believe the maître d' had no idea where he had placed your shawl? The old, tottering fool. It took him a full five minutes to locate it. How absurd! Anyway, here you are, my dear. Maybe next time you'll listen to me."

Lady Pemberton resumed her seat, asked a waiter for another cup of tea, then barged back into the conversation.

"So, what did I miss?" she asked.

I reclined in my chair and retracted my emotions within myself.

I had grown skilled at this over the years, out of necessity. Now composed, I answered Lady Pemberton.

"I was just asking Lady Kaylock about her career in opera," I stated.

"Oh yes, Victoria," the lady answered proudly. "Tell Mr. Grey about your latest role. Oh, Mr. Grey, it's the role of a lifetime!"

Victoria took a sip of her coffee, then lowered her cup and with detachment answered, "I have been asked to play the role of Brünnhilde in Wagner's *Twilight of the Gods* at Her Majesty's Theatre, beginning next week."

"Oh, isn't it marvelous?" Lady Pemberton broke in. "Victoria is one of the most graceful singers they've ever had! Why, the *Times* stated that, regardless of ridiculous ideas of disrepute in the profession, our Victoria could very well be the next Moran-Olden! What do you think of *that*, Mr. Grey? Our Victoria is becoming quite the luminary of stage and show!"

I raised my coffee in a mild toast toward Victoria, who only stared down at her hands in her lap.

"Congratulations, Lady Kaylock. That caliber of role is indeed impressive. It isn't given lightly. You must be delighted."

There was something in Victoria's expression that I just could not comprehend. I had never seen her so downcast and dispirited. *Strange.*

"Oh, of course," she replied unenthusiastically. "Father is excessively proud, and this is the career opportunity of a lifetime, even with the outrageous reputes of others in this field. Father believes it will keep the Kaylock name in the press."

Experiencing the sudden desire to encourage and console her, but unsure of what to say, I leaned in to provide support.

"I'm . . . quite sure that whatever you do will be rewarding and that you will excel at it."

Victoria raised her face finally to meet my gaze, and in her eyes I made out a hint of hope, although I was still unclear as to what was particularly upsetting her.

"She will perform brilliantly," Lady Pemberton broke in, "and the stage has never witnessed a more beautiful Brünnhilde."

"I'm eager to read your review in the *Times*. I'm sure it will be stellar," I said.

"Thank you," Victoria finally answered, still uncharacteristically timid.

"Mr. Grey," Lady Pemberton interjected, "forgive me, but might I ask you a particular question?"

Knowing full well the woman would ask regardless of my answer, I said nothing but awaited her query.

"Well, it's not so much a question as a matter of woman's intuition. I'd say there appears to be some type of interest between you and Lady Kaylock here. Perhaps you were entertaining the idea of *courting* her?"

"Roxanne!" Victoria blurted out, her face an instant shade of deep crimson.

"Oh, come now," Lady Pemberton unflinchingly continued. "You know your secret would be safe with me, and I would never hold judgment in this matter. Besides, Victoria is *long* overdue for a strong masculine figure in her life. I dare say I was beginning to wonder whether she would join a convent with how disinterested she has been with men's attentions since her last suitor—"

"Roxanne, that's enough!" Victoria exclaimed, even redder than before. "Ash—Mr. Grey—and I are . . . Well, we haven't . . . I mean to say—"

"We are acquaintances from childhood," I offered in an attempt to bail Victoria out. "We just recently were reacquainted after some years."

"That's right! We were playmates is all!" she added eagerly.

Lady Pemberton's mouth stretched into a wicked smile.

"Oh, I'll *bet* you were."

"Oh!" Victoria squealed, covering her mouth with her hands.

"Tell me, Mr. Grey," Pemberton continued, "will you come to

see Victoria perform? Perhaps a private performance for *two*? That *is* how many in the operatic circles do it, isn't it?"

Now I was perturbed and uncomfortable at Lady Pemberton's line of questioning. It was rude, even by my standards.

"Thank you, ladies, for a lovely evening," I said as I rose from my place at the table. "Lady Kaylock, I wish you all the best in your endeavors in the opera. Lady Pemberton, good night."

I bowed respectfully and turned to leave. Behind me, I heard Victoria hissing at Lady Pemberton as the redhead laughed the same laugh as when I first saw her.

My mind swam in currents of confusion, embarrassment, and irritation, making me feel vulnerable in a way I detested. I hastily exited Wendell's and burst into the night air. As I hailed a coach, I endeavored to tear my mind free of Victoria and all that was discussed and focus instead on the case.

It was getting late, and All Hollows' was drawing nigh. I had to discover what the Thirteenth Pentacle was up to; I had to be sure of whether they were truly a threat.

Climbing into the hansom, I gave the coachman the address, and he whipped the horses into motion. I steeled myself for what lay ahead. As I did, I thought I heard the voice of Victoria, calling my name. I shook my head to clear such distractions and waited anxiously for my hansom to take me straight into the lions' den: Vauxhall Gardens.

CHAPTER 7

To Seek Out a Cult

In the spirit of full disclosure, I think it only fair to further explain my brief stint in Her Majesty's army. I actively fought in England's Second Afghan War, which left a lasting impression upon me and whereby I acquired a suitable repertoire of skills in combat, firearms, survival, and, most valuable in this instance, the ability to move unseen behind suitable cover.

The other talents I picked up as a member of Her Majesty's Highlanders would come in handy later.

As I hunkered down in a hedge row at the edge of the Vauxhall Gardens' entryway, I was relatively confident I had not been seen making my approach. The coach had dropped me a block away after passing over Vauxhall Bridge. I crept to the gardens on foot from there, taking every precaution to stay tight to the shadows.

Already I had witnessed too much activity for my comfort. Over a dozen personal carriages had come in from the road and traveled down the cobblestone walkway leading deep into Vauxhall Gardens proper. There was no attempt to conceal the carriages' arrival. I could only deduce that this brazenness was due to the remote location and late hour—although possibly the arrogance of the Thirteenth Pentacle as well. From the looks of the private coaches, the group's membership consisted of the gentry or other people of means.

I strained to see where the carriages were heading but failed to discern much in the darkness over that great distance.

I had to draw nearer.

Discovering an evenly spaced line of fir trees to my right, I darted low and fast to the nearest, then to the next and the next, following the tree column across the expansive tract of the gardens. Fortunately, the tree line stretched parallel to the cobblestone road on which the carriages traveled, making it painless to track the cult members.

After traversing quite a distance, I arrived at a château illuminated from within by dozens of candles. Their yellow light glowed from high-arched windows on three levels.

From my vantage behind a sagging fir tree, I could just make out each carriage driving up to the covered entry of the great house. What appeared to be a steward, adorned in black and wearing a mask, opened each carriage door to let one or several passengers out. Every passenger was covered in a hooded, black, velvety cloak that completely hid their identities. They all wore similar masks, smooth and white with only black holes for their eyes. The steward aided them in disembarking.

These guests made their way inside without delay.

I pulled my pocket watch from my waistcoat. In the dim evening light, I perceived it was almost midnight.

As I put away my watch, a flicker of movement to my left caught my eye. I ducked low and peered at the line of fir trees I had just used as cover across the gardens. For a moment, nothing stirred, and I believed myself to be imagining things in my state of heightened alertness. Just when I was about to turn back toward the château to plan my approach, there was a sudden but brief movement two trees back from where I had come.

I was being followed.

Feeling my heart rate accelerate, I gritted my teeth and darted around the trunk I was using for cover, then ran fleetly toward the château's eastern wall. It was densely lined with tall standing pine trees. I made it to the wall easily enough under this degree of cover and darkness, then crouched into a narrow space between the high wall of the house and a particularly thick pine. And I watched, waiting to catch a glimpse of my pursuer.

The individual tracking me emerged from the fir trees, following the same route I had taken. Astonishingly, this mysterious follower in a hooded stole was a woman; I could identify her attempt to hold up the hem of her skirt as she ran. My stomach lurched with dread and irritation when it occurred to me precisely who this was.

As the woman reached the side of the château, it was clear that she had lost sight of me in the gloom because she ran in front of me and huddled against the side of the house, her back to me. I hung my head in exasperation for a moment. Then, stealthily, I crept up behind the crouched figure and swiftly wrapped my arm around her waist to lift her from the ground while placing my hand over her mouth to keep her from crying out.

The woman let out a muffled squeal, violently squirming and kicking her legs.

I spun her away from the house and attempted to whisper in her ear to remain calm, but before I could, a sudden pain shot through my fingers. She was biting my hand.

"Ugh! Victoria!" I grunted angrily but quietly.

Victoria Kaylock wrestled free from my grasp and, spinning about to face me, looked into my face with growing recognition.

"Ash? What are you doing?"

"Keep your voice down," I whispered, rubbing my fingers. "I was about to ask *you* the same question. What are you doing here? This is no place for you. It's dangerous."

Before Victoria could respond, a shadow passed over as a figure filled the arched window nearest us. Instinctively, I pulled Victoria toward me to press both of our backs against the wall, just out of sight of the window.

We both held our breath, hoping against hope that we had not been detected. When the shadow disappeared and several moments had passed without incident, I slowly exhaled, and Victoria did as well.

I leaned in close to her ear. "I don't know why you followed me, but you need to leave *immediately*."

"I'm not leaving without you. Don't think I'm some helpless little girl, Ash. I can watch out for myself. Anyway, with how reckless you've always been, you need me."

"Um, excuse me?"

"You need me to watch your back."

I sighed unintentionally. This was something I did not have the time for. The Thirteenth Pentacle was assembling within, giving me no time to squabble like we were children again.

"I do not like this, but we are out of time. Follow me and do exactly as I tell you. Understood?" I demanded.

Victoria nodded profusely, exhilaration filling her wide eyes. She pulled her cape closer and the hood lower.

"Stay low. Follow me," I whispered.

Bent low, we sidled down the length of the château wall to its rear corner.

An earlier glance through one of the arched windows had revealed an immense ballroom-like chamber in which the cult members appeared to be congregating. Across the upper level of the room, a wraparound balcony looked down upon the main floor—a perfect position from which to observe.

In the rear of this palatial manor, we discovered a solid latticework climbing the height of the house. Within arms' reach from the lattice was a small window by which we could access the balcony.

With no one in sight, we moved to the bottom of the lattice. I simply raised a finger, pointing up. It took a moment, and then Victoria lifted her head to inspect the lattice.

"You can't be serious," she gasped.

"I am," I answered, straightening to commence the ascent. "Or you can stay here if you prefer. Alone."

"Ugh. Fine," she grunted in frustration. "Stand aside."

Victoria grasped the lattice and slowly began to climb, heavy skirts and all. She had ascended some four to five heads above me before I began to scale the lattice as well.

"I'm almost to the window," Victoria whispered. "And, Ash, you had better not be taking any liberties by peering up my skirt."

"Don't flatter yourself, Victoria. Just climb," I quipped in return.

I had no clue as to why Victoria had followed me here, nor what she hoped to accomplish from it. From what little I gathered from our brief interaction in Wendell's, I wondered if Victoria's current life circumstances might not be as fulfilling as one might believe.

"I believe I can undo the latch on this window," Victoria said. "I just need a moment to work it free."

Hanging precariously beneath her as she worked on our means of entry, I took a brief look about to confirm that there was no one on the ground nearby who might discover us. The night had taken a sudden dip in temperature, reminding me of the autumnal time of year. Wisps of my breath surrounded me in the darkness. I saw no one, so I returned my attention to Victoria above me.

"How are you managing?" I asked.

"Almost," she mumbled, followed by an audible click. "I have it!"

"Get inside. Hurry now," I encouraged.

Victoria lifted her petite frame into the small window, vanishing into the gloom. I hoisted myself the remainder of the way and clambered into the window with relative ease. Inside, I found Victoria awaiting me in the duskiness of what looked to be a storage closet littered with furniture under tarps, antique paintings, and several statues. I brushed myself off absently and moved to a door at the far end of the room that should lead us into the chateau's interior.

"Why did you follow me?" I asked Victoria quietly while checking to see if the door was locked. "Why put yourself in this manner of mortal danger? You're an opera performer."

The door was unlocked. I turned the latch slowly and eased the door open a minuscule degree.

I heard Victoria shift behind me. "I'll still be a singer after tonight."

Peeking out through the crack, I spied that, to our good fortune, the door opened directly into a back corner of the balcony. I opened the door fully and gestured for Victoria to follow.

"To be honest, I was not a little surprised at the news that you had decided to join the opera," I confessed.

She stepped to the door. "And why is that? Do you not believe I am capable? Or do you believe my chosen occupation to be too scandalous for a proper lady?"

"Oh no. No, I know that your reputation was never something you were concerned about. And I am fully aware you can do anything you set your mind to. No, I was surprised because you were always so much more—"

"Unrefined?" she cut in defensively.

"Vivacious," I corrected. "I always believed something as droll as opera would bore you to tears." I took one last glance about, then, crouching low, extended my hand to Victoria. "Let's go. Stay low."

She blushed in hesitancy, then took my hand. Moving in a hunkered fashion, we crept out of the room and, staying in the shadows, took up a position where we could peer down upon the many gathered below us.

Beneath our hiding place, the immense ballroom was covered in dark wood paneling that appeared nearly black in the waxy light of the more than dozen candelabras surrounding its perimeter. The floors boasted an onyx polish, and the entire space smelled of a foreign spice or resin I could not quite place. Perhaps frankincense.

At the center of the ballroom was a table, black as well and in the shape of a horseshoe. Seated in dark, high-backed wooden chairs lining the entire table were about a dozen robed and masked figures. The chamber was lined with many more figures in robes—a surprising number of possibly one hundred or more. I took notice that the masks of those seated boasted an element that those of the standing crowd did not possess; they were smooth and white like the rest, but these masks bore the Roman numerical XIII etched upon the forehead. *Thirteen.*

All of those in attendance were silent and particularly attentive to an individual who sat at the center of the U-shaped table. Just as I leaned forward to get a clearer view of the man, he stood, allowing me the opportunity to inspect him easily.

"Faithful!" he began, his voice a deep baritone. "We stand upon the very precipice of a new world. For too long we have hidden away from the light, as we have combed the empire—yes, even the *world* over—for those sacred relics of our Master, to usher forth his fiery coming! But no longer!"

"Rejoice!" the entire audience responded in unison, causing Victoria to flinch and grab hold of my arm.

"Henceforth, the world will be eternally changed, and we, the Thirteenth Pentacle, ardent followers of the Pale King, will on All Hollows' at last make way for his advent! Robed in balefire! The direful and forbidding Samhain!"

"Rejoice! Rejoice!" the cultists universally responded.

The leader was charismatic, to be sure, but my discernment made the hair on the back of my neck stand upright. This man was undeniably linked to an infernal source, and his influence over his followers produced a palpable magnetism.

Thin in build, he was draped in a crimson robe with black embroidery resembling flames—or balefire, probably. He was hooded like the others and wore a mask resembling a demon of some type, preventing me from learning more about his identity. I *could* deduce, however, that the man was advanced in years from the raspiness of his voice and his choice of language.

Victoria whispered in my right ear, "That man, his voice sounds familiar to me somehow."

"Yes?"

"I am convinced I have heard it before, yet I cannot place where," she said searchingly.

The deranged cult leader continued his oration.

"We have received favor from our king! Where we searched blindly and in vain for the tools in which to bring Samhain's flaming return, now he has seen fit to give us direction! A guide that has been the voice and compass leading us to our destiny!"

"Rejoice!" answered the Pentacle again.

This time, the man gestured toward something behind him. I leaned lower to my left and immediately was struck by two different things.

One was that the Thirteenth Pentacle had managed to obtain the complete set of the Samhain relics, as I beheld a bulky, oversized suit of crimson armor hanging from a thick wooden frame. It was ornately detailed and reeked of demonic malice. There was no way that it was of the earth.

However, the second thing I noticed was far more unsettling. Behind the cult leader, just over his left shoulder, stood one of the most curious women I have ever seen. She stood about the same height as Victoria and to my astonishment wore no mask. The woman had short-cropped white hair, despite being quite young in the face, and eerily *red* eyes.

My senses screamed like a wailing banshee, bringing all my faculties to overload. So, this was the fortune teller I had heard mentioned.

The leader referred to her as the Pentacle's guide. I was not sure who, or *what*, this fortune teller was, but that was not my immediate concern. Something far more important became undeniably clear to me in that instant: the Thirteenth Pentacle was a very real threat, and it had to be stopped.

I turned to Victoria, whose attention was solely focused on the screaming madman below.

"In just two more nights, our reign will dawn as this world bends the knee to a new king," the man continued. "He will burn away to cinders all those lowly, poor, weak, and destitute with his balefire!"

"Rejoice!" came the reply.

"And so, to marshal the Pale King's terrible appearing, we, his retainers, will provide for him one such lowly wretch to begin the culling!"

From the entrance hall of the château came two Pentacle cultists dragging a man between them. The man had been beaten, as was obvious from copious lacerations and bruises, and he was clothed in the rags of an urchin. He struggled, but in vain, as he was clearly exhausted and feeble. He was thrown to the floor in the center space of the horseshoe table.

"Wait, what are they going to do?" Victoria gasped at me.

This was unconscionable. I fought to keep my rising rage from pouring out as I deduced the cult's gruesome intent.

Five Pentacle cultists surrounded the prostrate beggar, each holding a small black pot in their hands. The nauseously familiar fishy aroma of whale oil filled the room.

"Oh no," I muttered.

Victoria tugged on my arm urgently.

"Ash, they can't! We can't allow them to do this to him. We must stop this!"

I looked about the room, desperate to provoke an idea or plan to thwart this despicable act. There was a small army beneath us, but there had to be something we could do.

Then, it struck me. The plan was absurd, but it was our only hope.

I looked at Victoria. "Stay here," I whispered.

Before she could respond, I hastened back to the storage room through which we had previously entered. With as much rapidity as I could muster, I nabbed every tarp I could and dragged them back to where Victoria hid.

She looked at me in bewilderment.

"I need you to use those stairs over there," I whispered, nodding toward the stairwell that connected the balcony to the ground floor.

"If my estimation is correct, it should emerge just behind that cult leader, near where that accursed armor is erected."

"But someone will surely see me," she answered.

"No. They'll be too distracted," I answered.

"By what?"

"By me," I replied. "Remain inside the stairwell. When you hear the shouting, I want you to slip out and steal a piece of that armor. Any piece. We *cannot* allow them to possess the complete set and perform their ghastly ritual."

Below, events were unfolding rapidly.

"Prepare the sacrifice!" the cult leader commanded.

The five Pentacle followers began to empty their pots of oil upon the hapless soul at their feet. He moaned in confusion and anguish as he was drenched.

"Hurry now!" I hissed to Victoria.

Scooping up her skirts, she darted to the stairs and began to make her way steadily down. I took a slow breath, gathered my tarps, and took a position at one end of the balcony, directly over a few candelabras.

"And now, Faithful, we light the pyre of our devotion! The conflagration for our Pale King, Samhain!"

Another cultist entered the chamber with a lit torch lifted high, in unholy reverence.

Now was the time. If I did not act, this poor man would most definitely lose his life.

I rose posthaste and, lifting one tarp over the balcony rail, let it drop directly upon one of the bulky candelabras. The heavy stand fell to the hard floor with a crash, stunning all in attendance and distracting the torch bearer from his task. Then, suddenly, the tarp erupted into flames from the candles still buried beneath it.

A cultist rushed to stomp out the flames, and many began screaming out in alarm. As they did, I moved down the balcony and dropped a tarp onto another candelabra, then further down to do it a third time. These met with the same results as the first, scattering the candles across the floor before bursting into flames.

In a matter of seconds, the château's ballroom became engulfed in fire. Screaming, panicked, and enraged Thirteenth Pentacle members scattered in all directions.

I prayed Victoria had followed my instructions, but my primary focus was on the fate of the derelict that was to be their victim. To my relief, the disoriented man had somehow managed to rise to his feet and, with his captures preoccupied, was stumbling toward the side entrance out of the ballroom.

A sigh of relief escaped my lips but tragically caught again in my throat when I heard the leader shouting, "Look! There! Above! Apostate above! Remove him, Faithful! Destroy him!"

I turned my head toward the source of the screaming and found myself staring straight into the terrible man's face. Evidently, in his rage at the defilement of their sacrifice, he had taken off his mask. As I had suspected, he was elderly, presumably in his early seventies, with oiled-back white hair and thick sideburns. He was clean shaven, and his eyes held a fire of hatred that sent a quiver through my body.

Next to him, the fortune teller peered up at me as well, but despite her otherworldly eyes, her face held a different expression than that of her master. There was recognition there. She *knew* me. She knew me and was incensed.

That's when I realized that all of the cultists were staring up at me, and with a deafening roar that seemed to shake the balcony on which I stood, every last one of them cried out for my blood.

I hastily turned to run, glancing below one last time to see if I could catch a glimpse of Victoria anywhere. To my dismay, I saw no trace of her, but before I had the chance to panic, I heard her yell my name.

"Ash! This way!" Victoria screamed, standing in the open doorway that led back into the storage room.

I dashed toward the doorway as Victoria disappeared within, the screams and stomping feet of approaching mad cultists following close behind me. When I reached the small window at the rear of the room, I discovered Victoria had already clambered outside and had begun the descent.

"Tell me you managed to recover a section of that armor," I exclaimed while swinging myself out the window and onto the lattice.

"I *told* you I could watch out for myself!" she whooped.

I glanced beneath me and saw Victoria waving an ornate steel gauntlet in one hand and clutching the lattice with the other.

"You need me!" she boasted.

We did not have time for this. I gritted my teeth to fight off a coarse reply and focused on making my way down the latticework as hastily as possible. Above, the cultists shouted upon discovering the room and our means of escape.

Victoria hopped to the grass below, and I reached the ground only a moment later.

"Well," she said with a smirk, "are you still upset that I followed you?"

Before I could respond, the night was split by the loud crack of firearms above us. Several Pentacle cultists were leaning out the window overhead and firing pistols down upon us.

Victoria screamed in surprise. I grabbed her arm and pulled her with me.

"Run!" I yelled.

Together, we bolted across the open field toward the cover of the fir trees we had utilized as concealment when arriving at Vauxhall Gardens. The terrain about our running feet exploded with the impact of bullets, narrowly missing us. Somewhere to our rear, shouting erupted as more of the Pentacle engaged us in pursuit.

Finally reaching the first of the fir trees, we ducked behind it, and rounds thudded heavily into the trunk. Before we could break for the next tree, however, we were assailed by a cultist from our right, who blindsided me with a rapid punch to my jaw.

I stumbled but did not lose my footing, although the unexpected strike caused me to see stars and lose my grip on Victoria. The cultist swung a right hook, but this time I was ready. I ducked beneath his punch and countered with a blow to his stomach. When he doubled over, his jaw met with my knee as I brought it up to his face.

More gunfire erupted about us as the cultist slumped to the ground.

Victoria was panting wisps in the cold air, her eyes wide with panic.

"Move!" I yelled.

But Victoria's arm was seized by another cultist who had managed to catch up. He tugged at her brutally, determined to reclaim the stolen unholy relic.

"No!" she yelled angrily. "Let go!"

I dove forward, tackling the cultist in his middle body and sending us both sprawling to the grass. I saw the gauntlet wrenched free but kept my concentration on the adversary on the ground with me. Before he could recover, I climbed atop him and painfully headbutted the cultist through his mask.

My forehead thrummed, but I quickly regained my feet to see Victoria a few paces off, flinching away to her left as bullets struck the ground around her. To my amazement, she deftly pulled a revolver from within her dress, aimed with both hands, and fired once, then twice.

I did not have time to question where Victoria had obtained the weapon; my attention was on retrieving the lost gauntlet. Spotting it several paces away, I moved to grab the relic but was cut off by another valley of gunshots tearing up the turf and whipping through my coat.

"Come on, Ash!" Victoria shouted. "We must escape!"

"Not without the gauntlet!" I yelled.

Victoria fired again at the approaching attackers. "Forget that! Come on!" She grabbed my sleeve and pulling me with her.

I pushed down my discouragement at leaving the gauntlet behind and instead fled with Victoria. I could only spare one final, fleeting thought for the hapless sacrificial victim and hope that we'd provided all the distraction he needed. My belief was that he would disappear into the darkness of the London streets and out of the Pentacle's thoughts. Bullets whizzed past us while we dashed through the column of fir trees, weaving this way and that to present more difficult targets. Victoria kept pace with me, much more agile in her heavy skirts than I would have thought.

Finally, we reached the entrance to Vauxhall Gardens and the road itself. To my great relief and pleasure, we were greeted by Victoria's coach moving toward us with vigor.

"When I managed to edge away from Gerard and get to my coach tonight, I instructed my coachman to be on the ready until my return," Victoria exclaimed. Without reply, I hoisted her into the carriage, then lunged in as well.

"Go! Go!" I yelled.

The coachman snapped the horses into a gallop down the road. Shots rang out to our rear, sparking cobblestones and thudding into the wood of the carriage.

Then, before we knew it, we were rapidly heading back toward London and leaving Vauxhall Gardens behind us.

I looked across at Victoria, who, like me, was attempting to slow her breathing and compose herself. She had done nothing but surprise me this night, and I was impressed by her bravery and stalwartness in the face of so much danger. I wanted to tell her so, but the old wounds of the past stubbornly kept my words from coming out. Instead, I indulged my curiosity.

"Where did you get the gun?" I asked.

She held it up. It was a Smith & Wesson revolver, a .32 caliber American pistol, to my surprise.

"This? It . . . was a gift. From a former . . . suitor."

"I see. And the shooting? Did this 'suitor' teach you?"

"No. Father has taught me since, well, since a few years after you left."

I nodded and looked out the carriage window, suddenly uncomfortable. I changed the subject.

"I need to develop a new strategy," I said.

Victoria sighed, sounding annoyed. "Yes?"

"Well, since we lost the relic, I now need to invent a new method of leverage on the Thirteenth Pentacle."

"Lost?" she repeated.

"The gauntlet," I clarified.

Victoria reached into the folds of her cape lining and pulled out a crimson steel gauntlet, elaborate and grim. "Do you mean like this one?" she asked wryly, a smirk on her lips.

"What? I don't understand," I muttered, gently taking the piece of armor from her outstretched hand. It dawned on me. "You grabbed them both."

Victoria giggled and smiled proudly.

"It was simple enough. This cape has very large pockets."

I suddenly smiled, pleased with the turn of events and the quick thinking of my childhood friend.

Nonetheless, as my excitement and blood began to calm, a wave of weakness, nausea, and pain crashed over me. My ribs throbbed, and I unconsciously reached inside my coat to touch my side. Something was very wrong.

"Coachman! Pull over here!" I yelled out to the carriage driver.

We had just crossed back over Vauxhall Bridge and were driving through Whitehall toward Charing Cross. As the carriage stopped, I hurriedly disembarked and shut the door behind me to prevent Victoria from following.

"Ash, what are you doing?" she exclaimed.

"This is where we part ways. You need to return home where you're safe. There's something I need to see to."

"But I can help," she argued.

I shook my head resolutely.

"Not tonight," I answered, then addressed the coachman. "See she gets home safely."

He nodded. "Right you are, governor."

Victoria wore a mask of exasperation and disappointment but held her tongue as she gazed at me silently from the carriage window.

I looked at my feet. "I . . . didn't steal that broach, back then," I whispered. "I never would've done that, you know."

Victoria's eyes filled with emotion.

"I know," she whispered back.

The carriage burst into motion, rumbling down the dark avenue, and before I knew it, I was standing alone in the night of Whitehall.

I turned toward the many government buildings, their white marble ghostly in the moonlight. I took a step across the street and to my dismay stumbled weakly, clutching my ribs at another wave of pain.

I stared at my hand. It was soaked with blood.

I stumbled down one side street, holding my side and 97willing my body to continue before I passed out. Before long, I reached my destination: a nondescript, white marble building with two heavy iron doors bolted shut for the night.

I shuffled to the doors and, collapsing against them, managed to strike hard once before completely falling to the steps. I remember looking up at the night sky and marveling at the beauty of the stars that I was otherwise too busy to notice.

Then, all was black.

CHAPTER 8

Family Insights

LONDON

October 30

It has been some time since the events of that evening, but even as I pen this account, I can recall the dreams I had with utmost clarity.

Before me and behind me rose immense and grotesque black shadows, nondescript but overwhelmingly oppressive. I felt compelled to chase the one ahead of me, while at the same time equally compelled to escape the one behind. As I ran, all around me lay pumpkins, all lit from within with a flame that would not extinguish, a green flame.

There was overwhelming, cackling laughter. Then there were the eyes—crimson. The eyes of the fortune teller, who seemed to somehow know me, and I her.

Finally, I began to fall. It was the gut-clenching plummet backward that makes one's breath catch and heart race. A fall into nothing and nowhere.

I awoke.

My breathing heightened from my dreams, I lay staring at the ceiling, allowing my gasping to subside. The ceiling was an intricately designed baronial work, the type one would see in a palatial home or government edifice.

A voice, low and morose, addressed me from somewhere near my feet.

"You're finally awake."

As I lifted my head to look toward the voice, pain shot through my ribs, and I instantly recalled that I had been shot in the frantic bustle to escape with Victoria.

"How long have I been out?" I asked the voice.

"We found you around one o'clock or so in the morning, so, close to fifteen hours. It's October 30, at five in the evening," the voice answered. "You've made a right mess of yourself, haven't you, Ash?"

I pushed myself painfully to my elbows to gain a bearing on where I was.

"It's good to see you too, Nicholas," I said dryly.

At the end of the bed in which I reclined stood a large man resting his back against the wall. He had short brown hair with long sideburns, a square jaw, and easily stood a head taller than me. A clear expression of disappointment tinged with irritation graced his face.

"Pfft," he scoffed. "I had our in-house nurse tend to your bullet wound. It was not deep. Seems to have bounced off a rib, so no real damage was done. You've been sutured and bandaged. You're in quite a state. What are you involved in now, Ash?"

I managed to push into a sitting position, then slid a pillow behind me for support and scanned the room.

"Nothing more unusual than is common for me, little brother. Are we still in Whitehall? By the looks of the room—"

"Yes, yes. The butler found you on the front steps of the Diogenes Club and brought you up to my floor, per my orders," Nicholas interrupted. "And don't call me that."

Yes, Nicholas, or rather *Sir* Nicholas Grey of Her Majesty's Service, is my younger brother by four years, despite the clear difference in stature. We have never been close, as we are entirely different people. And Nic has never truly forgiven me for the matter with the Kaylocks, and for my running away. Needless to say, the years without me pushed his determination to make a name for himself, which he eventually did, being knighted by the queen herself.

That's a story for another time.

"What are you doing here, Ash?" he asked bluntly. Nicholas was always like that, straightforward and matter-of-fact.

"I was bleeding," I said flatly. "I assumed that was apparent."

"Yes, but why *else* are you here? What do you want?" he asked, crossing his arms over his chest.

I raised my eyebrows. "What gives you the impression I want anything from you, Nic? Can't a mortally wounded man come to his brother for care without being suspected of having an agenda?"

Just then, a maidservant entered the room, carrying a silver tray with several dishes atop it, as well as a copy of the *Times*.

"Oh! Forgive me, sir. It's just that now that the patient is awake, I thought he might like something to eat to replenish his strength," she stammered under Nicholas's gaze.

With an eye roll, he gestured for the woman to continue her duties and serve me the meal. I realized how famished I was as the delightful smells of yams, potatoes, and pork filled my senses. Though I attempted to be civil, I was ravenous and heartily dug into the meal—as one might expect of someone unconscious for a full day.

My brother sighed and moved to the window, straightening his pristine jacket as he did. He took up station looking outside, his thick arms clasped behind him. Nicholas was always adorned with the most expensive black suits and tuxedos, evidence of his position and station. There was very little on the man that was not starched and pressed.

I glanced his way, then resumed my meal, picking up the day's edition of the *Times*.

"So, what is it that you're working on these days? A lonely widow with a naughty ghost? Goblins in a family's wine cellar?"

I was accustomed to my brother's skepticism and apprehension about my work and therefore did not allow his dry sarcasm to stir my anger.

"Oh, just attempting to uncover the diabolical machinations of a devil-worshiping cult before they accomplish their plan to summon their demon god to earth. The usual. Why the sudden interest in my work? Don't tell me you're beginning to believe, dear brother?"

"Pfft. Hardly," Nicholas scoffed again. He had become a professional at hard-bitten cynicism over the years. "I'm merely curious as to what ghoul or witch would cause my older brother to be *shot*, is all. I believe that to be a very natural question."

"Cultists carry revolvers," I replied.

"Not *all* cultists, surely."

"These do."

Nicholas kept his back to me. His broad shoulders did not move, making it difficult to ascertain what he could be thinking.

"Perhaps you should leave these pistol-carrying fanatics to their clandestine meetings and orgies," he said sarcastically, "and find another case that requires less bloodshed and danger. Maybe a medium is purloining from her client somewhere?"

I continued to absently banter while perusing the *Times*' front page.

"Oh, I wouldn't dream of it. Not when I can put life and limb in mortal danger. Why, with all of the exercise I receive in fleeing for my life, it's done wonders for my constitution alone. In fact . . ." My sentence trailed off as my eyes fell upon a photo in the *Times*.

"Yes?" Nicholas answered. "In fact what?"

I did not answer. I could not.

I stared in horror at the photo: a stately elderly man with oiled white hair and a bare face—and somewhere nearby, I knew, although I could not see her in the photo, was a fortune teller. She had to be.

For on the front page of the *Times* was the face of the Thirteenth Pentacle cult leader, the man who wrathfully removed his mask as he screamed for my death. The same man who ordered a poor soul to be burned alive as an infernal sacrifice.

"Asher, what's the matter with you? You look as if someone just walked over your grave," Sir Nicolas queried.

I stared at my brother, my mind racing. I turned the front page over for him to see.

"Nicholas," I began, "what do you know about this man here, Sir Edward Rosemond?"

My brother strode heavily across the room to my bedside and took the paper from my hand. After glancing at it, he tossed it upon the blanket next to me.

"Sir Rosemond is an aristocrat from an old and wealthy family. He's a member of Parliament and has his fingers in varying facets within the empire and abroad," he rumbled. "Why? Who is he to you?" He narrowed his eyes suspiciously.

I glanced down at the newspaper beside me, attempting to grasp the ramifications of this discovery. *How did I miss this?* If the leader of the Thirteenth Pentacle was a gentleman member of the British Parliament, then I had truly underestimated the caliber of foe I was contending with.

"I saw him last night. He was the leader of the cult that nearly killed me," I said without lifting my head.

After a pause, Nicholas asked, "Are you certain of this?"

I glanced up at him quickly, taken off guard by his lack of surprise.

"Yes," I said firmly. "Why? You know something about him, don't you?"

Nicolas held his thick arms behind him once again and stepped back to gaze out the window. "Sir Rosemond has been of interest for some time," he said quietly.

My brother is thought by most of his acquaintances and the general public to be employed in a droll British government position within the endless clerical offices of Whitehall.

I know better.

In truth, Sir Nicholas Grey is under the vocation and headship of Scotland Yard's Special Branch, a clandestine department under the command of William Melville. Theirs is the task of rooting out the agendas and machinations of those groups who present a danger to the Crown, whether foreign or domestic.

Bluntly speaking, Nicholas is a spy. And if he suggested that Sir Edmund Rosemond was of "interest," then that implied Scotland Yard or others were aware of him.

"Interest?" I pressed.

He did not move—a slab of a man in a black tuxedo.

"Scotland Yard has suspected him of being at the epicenter of a hellfire club; we just have never uncovered enough evidence to confirm it."

I raised my arms dramatically to fully reveal my bandages and wounded side.

"Well, consider *this* confirmation!" I exclaimed.

My brother looked at me sideways and snorted.

"What transpired with you isn't enough to charge Rosemond. If we brought him in now, he would simply deny ever being there, and then conveniently supply a dozen witnesses to vouch for him. Besides, you can't even prove he was the perpetrator who shot you. No, he's much too clever to be apprehended in such a fashion."

I considered what my brother was telling me, and as much as I loathed it, I knew his deductions were correct. Although Sir Rosemond was the head of a "hellfire club," Scotland Yard's idiom for any high-society secret society, so were many other gentlemen and nobility in London. That in itself was not a prosecutable offense, and we had no substantial evidence to legally validate that the Thirteenth Pentacle was a threat to the Crown.

While contemplating this, Nicholas moved to a wardrobe on the far-right wall and opened it. I immediately recognized my clothes hanging within. From an inner drawer he removed the eerie Samhain gauntlet, its dark luster twinkling in a ghostly fashion.

"I'm assuming this belongs to Rosemond's group?" he asked.

I merely nodded.

"A component for the ritual, no doubt."

I again regarded my brother with surprise.

"Oh yes," he said in response to my reaction. "We are aware of Rosemond's attempts to enact his macabre 'rite.' He's been pursuing that mission for some years now, in fact. To no avail. The poor lunatic has never been able to locate all the components for his 'quest,'" Nicolas added in light condescension.

"Until now," I added.

"What?"

"Until now. He possesses them all now. Well, except that one there," I said, gesturing to the gauntlet in my brother's hands.

Nicholas's usually stoic and disinterested expression slipped for a moment, giving way to an expression of concern.

"Wait a moment, Asher. Are you stating that Rosemond has *all* of the armor segments?"

"I saw them all myself," I answered, not a little uneasy over his sudden interest.

"How is that possible?" he mumbled under his breath.

"The fortune teller," I answered.

"What? What fortune teller?"

"Sir Rosemond has had a fortune teller in his company, apparently. It was she who helped him discover the missing pieces. There is something malevolent about her."

"Please, Ash, that will be enough of that nonsense. We may have a very real threat here. Not to say that I believe anything regarding Rosemond's ritual ever truly producing results, but an empowered cult makes for a far more dangerous one."

I shook my head. "I felt what I felt. Regardless, I heard Rosemont give credit for the discovery of the armor to this fortune teller myself."

Nicholas regained his typical glum composure and returned the gauntlet to the wardrobe with the rest of my belongings. He resumed his position at the foot of my bed, his arms behind his back once again.

"Ash, I think it may be prudent for you to recuse yourself from this affair."

"You know I can't do that."

"Don't be an imbecile," he said bluntly. "If Rosemond is as dangerous as we fear, you need to keep a wide berth from him and his lackeys. Good God, Ash, you've already been shot! You could very well be *killed* next time. Now, I insist you stop being so obstinate and leave this in the hands of Scotland Yard and Her Majesty's government!"

I moved aside the bed linens and swung my legs off the edge of the bed. The wood floor was cold on my feet. I shook my head dismissively.

"That's impossible, I'm afraid," I replied.

Nicholas groaned in frustration.

"At least leave the gauntlet in my care," he insisted, "to be sure it's not going to fall into Rosemond's hands."

I shuffled painfully to the wardrobe, my side protesting, and began to gather my clothes and get dressed. Nicolas clenched his square jaw and shook his head with aggravation.

I knew deep down that my brother cared for my well-being, but I could not sit idle and expect others to tend to matters, especially the constabulary of Scotland Yard. Not to state that some did not perform admirably in their duties, but there was no time to wait for the Yard to gather evidence and make arrests. All Hallows' Eve was tomorrow.

Nicolas stood aside as I put on my waistcoat and reached for my overcoat.

"If you have the gauntlet, you do know they will be coming for you," he stated matter-of-factly.

"I know," I replied. Having donned my overcoat, I retrieved the piece of crimson armor. "But I would much rather they be hounding me and not someone else."

I opened the door to the room and looked at my brother one more time.

"My thanks for patching me up," I stated genuinely, patting Nicholas on his big shoulder, "little brother."

He snorted in derision, shaking his head.

As I exited, contemplating a strategy in dealing with the Thirteenth Pentacle, Nicholas's voice follow me down the corridor: "Don't call me that."

The sun was already well down as I took the carriage from Whitehall back to my flat on Knight's Street. The sky overhead was a foreboding violet, tinged with a creeping black cloud front.

Carriage wheels rumbled, and horse hooves clopped upon cobblestone. It did not take long for me to comprehend my discernment shouting at me that something was extremely amiss—a nameless fear that something terrible had happened.

I could not place it, but it was as if my heart were steadily rising in my chest, threatening to breach from within my throat. A very palpable tension surged, and I commanded the coachman to move the hansom with haste.

By the time I arrived in front of my Knight's Street flat, my pulse had reached a rapid percussion. I flung the payment to my coachman and galloped to the front door, which, to my growing anxiety, I found open—clearly by force, as the door was hanging by one brass hinge.

I eased through the open doorway, moving with guarded wariness. Inside my flat, everything was quiet and dark. I nudged my way into the inner hall and stood unmoving at the base of the stairs, listening. When I was sure there was no one moving about, I proceeded to the second floor, where I discovered my bedroom in shambles, torn asunder in a brutal search.

Rosemond had sent someone in search of the Samhain gauntlet; yet how did they discover who I was, much less where I lived?

Then it occurred to me.

The fortune teller.

The previous night in Vauxhall Gardens, when that strange woman saw me on the balcony, I recalled her expression. She knew me somehow. She knew who I was. From there, it would be easy to discover where I resided.

I moved up the stairs again to my third-floor study to find the door ajar there as well. This time, however, all was not dark. A single lit candle flickered at the center of the room, as it had on Sabina's visit. Bookshelves were toppled, and my desk's contents were strewn across the floor. Various papers, trinkets, and even stuffing from the few chair cushions were liberally scattered.

My attention was not upon any of these distractions but on something pinned on the small table with the candle. Something golden pinned with a knife.

As I drew close, I was filled with perhaps the greatest feeling of revulsion and dread I had ever experienced. The bile rose in my stomach, and I had to force it down.

There, staked to the table by the long, thin dagger, was a thick lock of golden hair.

Underneath was a note:

WE WANT THE HAND
MIDNIGHT
PLEASURE GARDEN
SOUTH BANK, THAMES

My vision went out of focus at the horror that filled my heart. I could not breathe.

The Thirteenth Pentacle had kidnapped Victoria.

CHAPTER 9

Snake Pit

LONDON

October 30

There is a particular degree of fear that, when experienced, swells up within the stomach and grips the very heart of a man. Dread, some call it. The body perspires, the pulse quickens, and the appetite is lost. The potency of that brand of trepidation can be debilitating or outright paralyzing.

I struggled against all of my body's instincts to shut down, fall apart, and give up. I threw myself into a coach, and, leaving my ransacked flat behind, traveled at great speed to the Pleasure Gardens on the South Bank.

Traveling northeast from Knight's Street, I watched the South London night blur by as my mind conjured up every conceivable fear regarding Victoria's safety. *Is she injured? What are these madmen putting her through? Is she even still alive?* I shook my head violently to clear such morbid ideas. The terror over unknowns and uncontrollable events would not benefit me in retrieving Victoria. I pushed them down and attempted to ascertain how the Thirteenth Pentacle managed to apprehend Victoria.

What do I know? The Thirteenth Pentacle knew exactly who I was, thanks to that strange fortune teller. It was well within the realm of possibility that someone within the Pentacle had recognized

Victoria simply from her social status as a rising luminary in London. The Pentacle membership was comprised mostly of aristocrats probably well acquainted with theater.

Blast! I should've known better than to let my emotions cloud my judgment. I should never have allowed Victoria to accompany me at Vauxhall, and I should have taken greater precautions at protecting her identity. Most likely, her hansom had been ambushed after I left her to be taken home.

Regardless of how, Rosemond had Victoria now.

The night had turned, and I felt rain in the air as the wind picked up and battered against my rapidly moving coach. The sky was completely black except for a flash of distant lightning on the horizon.

An ominous weight filled my heart, so I ground my teeth and focused on the task at hand. The carriage slowed and came to a stop outside an iron fence surrounding an open demesne that was dissected by a long gravel road. Full, thick trees lined both sides of the road, which was more of a walkway than a wider lane for hansoms or carts. There was no visible sign of anyone.

No *visible* sign.

My discernment was screaming at the sense of oppression in this place—a heaviness of supernatural origin, most likely demonic. I was very aware I was in danger, although I did not need any type of discernment to know that.

Paying for the cab and sending him on, I strolled up the gravel path, further into Pleasure Gardens. The trees waved and shifted around me, sighing as the wind bent them to and fro. Leaves blowing across the path toppled end over end like hundreds of pinwheels.

I kept my eyes open for other movement. Of course it was a trap, and unavoidable; I knew that. But it was always wise to keep a sharp edge—to never be taken off balance any more than necessary.

My hand continued to finger the item under my coat, the only real leverage I had: the gauntlet of the Pale King. It oozed wickedness, and part of me wanted to be rid of the infernal thing in any way I could.

As I moved down the path toward the waterline of the Thames, I spotted a ruin silhouetted by the lights across the river. It stood jagged and villainous, a black crown of towers. There was no movement or light within, but I knew instinctively that I had reached my destination. Whatever awaited me, it would be here.

Approaching the ruin, I realized it comprised what remained of a large hall that looked to have met its end by fire. The skeletal parapets were still visibly scorched. I stopped short of the ruin's high open gate and let my eyes trace my surroundings. There was still no sign of movement save the wind, which produced audible breathing and groaning from the ruin itself.

Cautiously, I stepped inside and made my way down a lengthy, open-air corridor. The ruins smelled of dirt, decaying wood, and rainwater. As I reached the end of the passage, I discovered it opened into a wide inner courtyard.

As I mentioned previously, since the time of my death and subsequent resurrection, I have had the displeasure of encountering a menagerie of characters ranging from bizarre to diabolical. Among those are individuals in whom there is not and need not be a demonic presence in order to inspire heinous acts of greed and despicableness. Such men are wicked on their own, driven by twisted and perverted ambitions.

I knew the moment I faced Edward Rosemont in personal proximity that he was such a man.

Striding into the courtyard, I saw the Thirteenth Pentacle leader at the far end. He no longer wore the robe or mask of the cult; instead, he wore a fashionable black suit and tie, his oiled, white hair stark against the black ruins. Pulled tightly against his left side, with one hand on her shoulder to hold her in place, was Victoria, looking disheveled and unnerved. Her beautiful golden hair hung haphazardly about her face, which was pink and smeared with grime. It was easy to deduce that she had put up a fight.

Rosemond squeezed her shoulder as I approached, and she

winced. Rage built in my belly, desperate anger and an all-consuming desire to see her safe. But I had to stay composed and focused. It would help no one if I gave in to emotion now.

To Sir Rosemond's right stood the man's constant companion, the fortune teller with her short hair and red eyes. She stared at me knowingly but without expression, whereas Rosemond wore a grin of confidence and victory.

Once I reach the center of the open courtyard, Rosemond raised his free hand.

"That will be quite close enough, Mr. Grey," he stated. "We can see and hear one another right here. Now we can have a little chat."

"Intriguing locale you've chosen, Sir Rosemond," I replied, allowing him to know that I knew his identity as well as he knew mine. "Intriguing, that is, for a kidnapping."

A forced chuckle emerged from the elderly gentleman, his grin now mixed with irritation. He glanced at the fortune teller. "Oh, he *is* an irreverent one, isn't he? No small wonder you've become taken with him. He's just as you described."

The fortune teller's eyes narrowed, seeming to glint with pleased and mischievous contentment. "Yes," she said. "I look forward to finally *breaking* him."

Her voice sent a chill down my spine—but not because it instilled me with fear. I had witnessed far too much to allow that to shake me. No, I was struck by the fortune teller's voice because, somehow, I recognized it. I did not know how or from where, but she was familiar to me.

I pulled my thoughts back to where they belonged: rescuing Victoria.

"Let the lady go, Rosemond. You've summoned me here successfully, and I brought your prize." I removed the gauntlet of the Pale King from my overcoat and held it in front of me. "Lady Kaylock is no longer necessary," I continued. "Release her, and you can take your prize."

Sir Rosemond scanned Victoria for a moment. For a brief instant, I believed he might release her, but that thought was immediately abandoned when he returned his gaze to mine and sneered.

"Mr. Grey, you're in no position to negotiate. I do believe you have underestimated the predicament you are in."

At his words, scores of dark silhouettes stepped forth from all around the courtyard, as well as above, in the encircling walls and parapets.

"Now then," Rosemond said condescendingly, "give us the relic, Mr. Grey. I have neither the time nor the patience to have any further dealings with the likes of you."

I knew my situation to be futile; there was simply no way to overpower this many adversaries, even with my considerable abilities. I could only stall and hope an opportunity for escape presented itself.

I endeavored to appeal to his vanity. "This summoning business, it's a bit below someone of your station and calling, is it not?"

Sir Rosemond looked perturbed.

"This 'summoning,' as you call it, *is* my calling. I have the highest honor of being the harbinger and herald of the Pale King! Politics and Parliament are but a means to an end. Soon, the whole empire will bend the knee to a new king, one whose reign will usher in shadow and balefire, and we his faithful will rule as the world burns! Now, Mr. Grey, give us the relic, or we will cut you down and pry it from your lifeless fingers. Choose!"

I knew I was without an option. For as desperately as I wanted to both save Victoria and keep the gauntlet from the Pentacle's hands, I could only hope that giving up one would allow me to save the other.

Extending my hand, I looked at the armor piece for a moment, hesitating in my internal struggle.

"*Now*, Mr. Grey! I will not hesitate to break the neck this beautiful face rests upon!" Rosemond commanded. He gripped Victoria's neck from behind, forcing a gasp from her lips.

Clenching my teeth in frustration, I tossed the gauntlet at the feet of the insane aristocrat.

Sir Rosemond smiled victoriously and with a jerk of his head sent the fortune teller to stoop and pick up the relic. She held it like an infant child. It made me sick. Another cultist, this one masked, rushed over and relieved the fortune teller of the load, wrapping it tenderly in a cloth and then withdrawing again amongst the others in the darkness.

"Well, now," Rosemond began almost cheerfully, "for as entertaining as this has been, I must be departing. There is much to be done and very little time, I'm afraid. Goodbye, Mr. Grey."

"Wait!" I yelled. "You have everything you want. Allow Lady Kaylock to go free. She is of no use to you now."

"Oh, but you see, that is where you're mistaken. We are still in need of a sacrifice to complete the ritual, and I have never encountered a more beautiful and suitable one than she."

Victoria screamed and struggled to break free, but several cultists jumped to aid their master by grabbing her and dragging her away.

"No! Ash! Ash!" she cried.

"And now," Rosemond sneered, looking at the fortune teller, "he's all yours."

The wicked woman grinned then—a high, feral grin, like some kind of predatory animal—and began to pace toward me. Rosemond and the rest of the Pentacle withdrew, dragging a screaming Victoria with them into the black of the night.

I peered about and noticed three other cultists had remained, encircling me, along with the fortune teller. They moved in, tightening the circle, drawing ever closer.

"I've been awaiting this chance, Asher Grey. Waiting to see this look on your face of confusion and fear just before your end," the fortune teller hissed. "I told you before, you are but a pebble to be kicked aside by the mighty and terrible, Rekindled One."

Recognition set in. I had experienced the sensation that I had met this individual before because I had. Just not in her current body.

She must have deciphered my expression of comprehension; she grinned even wider—the grin of a snake.

"Ah, *there* it is. Only at your finish do you finally understand," she jeered.

I spread my feet, preparing for an attack. "I should've known a simple expulsion exorcism wouldn't be enough for an Apepi demon," I said in a low voice. "At least George Brand is free of you. And who is this poor soul you're riding about in now?"

The woman scoffed carelessly. "Oh, this woman? This woman is a willing vessel. She *invited* me in!"

Suddenly, from my right, one of the cultists lunged toward me. I spun rapidly, utilizing his momentum against him and sending him careening past me. As he did so, though, I recognized something that caused a catch in my breath. His eyes, barely visible through the slits in his mask, were red.

The cultist toppled heavily onto the turf, and I studied the others as best I could: not one but *four* Apepi demoniacs. I raised my hands to prepare for the next assault.

The lead demon inside the fortune teller snarled, "Tear him apart! Do not allow him to grab ahold of you!"

Smarter than the average demon too, hmm? It knew I could expel it physically if I gained a grip on it. It remembered its defeat at my hand.

With a shriek, a cultist to my right leaped forward, his hands extended toward my face. I ducked, punching him hard in the belly. When he doubled over, I kicked him in the jaw. His mask flipped off as he fell backward.

The first cultist came at me again, tackling me solidly in the midsection. My breath was knocked from my lungs as I fell backward onto the dirt. He flung hands with jagged broken nails at my face, and I clutched his wrists firmly to keep them from tearing my flesh.

The other cultists were converging upon me. I knew I had to act without delay.

Jabbing my head forward, I smashed my forehead into the

man's mask. Once, then again. After the third time, the mask split, revealing a red-eyed and bloodied face beneath. Feeling him weaken for a moment, I kicked up with my legs, sending my attacker flipping head over heels clear of me.

I swiftly regained my feet and realized I was bleeding as well, from a gash on my forehead. There was no time to allow distraction, however. The third cultist's fist connected with my face solidly before I saw it coming. My head spun, and I took another hit in my ribs. Something cracked, but before I could catch my breath, the cultist's hands were around my throat.

I heard the cackling laughter of the demon I remembered so well from back in Bedlam. With all my strength, I thrust one hand up between the demoniac cultist's arms, catching him solidly in the forehead.

His red eyes gleamed at me beneath his mask, and he hissed menacingly.

I continued to push, using the gifting given to me upon my resurrection by the Almighty. Inside the cultist, the Apepi demon fought desperately, struggling to remain within his victim. I thrust my hand harder still, almost out of breath and on the verge of losing consciousness. Flickers of blue lightning began to ripple up my arms.

From the back of the cultist's head emerged the screaming Apepi demon, serpentine and nauseating green in color. Just as I had several nights earlier at Bedlam, in the exorcism of George Brand, I pushed with everything my constitution could bring to bear. The demon's slitted pupils widened as I quite literally pushed it from its victim's body and away from the physical plane.

Rapidly dissolving from the legs upward, the Apepi bellowed one long wail, then abruptly vanished from view.

The Apepi fortune teller and the other two demoniacs that were attempting to recover from their first assault joined together in a unified lament, I assumed out of rage from one of their own being removed from the fight.

I had only expelled the demon, not fully exorcised it, which meant, like the demon in the fortune teller, it could return in a different host. To fully exorcise them, I would need time, and that was in short supply.

The screams of the cultists did give me the time I required to regain my feet, however, and this time, I brought the fight to them. Promptly closing the distance between myself and the nearest cultist, I spun him around to get behind him and wrapped my arms around his head and neck, locking him in place and forcing him to gasp for air.

With the few moments that gave me, I pressed my hand hard against the man's back. Blue lightning arced. The demon inside hissed menacingly, realizing what was about to happen. Propelled by my hand, it emerged out of the cultist's chest and stomach, shrieking, flailing its deformed arms wildly about, seeking a handhold.

Then, just before the fiend was expelled, a sudden, sharp pain shot through my lower back. I gasped and released the demoniac, then realized that I had been clawed by the other cultist, who had recovered faster than I anticipated. I stumbled to one knee but managed to deflect a kick aimed at my skull. The demoniac kicked again, and I parried that one as well, and this time delivered a quick jab to his chest in return.

This stunned him, granting me an opening to launch to my feet and bring both fists down upon his head, knocking the sense out of him.

I confess that at this point, I was angry. I reached down to the cultist's back and, wrapping my fingers into a fist at the base of his neck, physically gripped the Apepi demon inside, then tugged upward with as much force as I could muster.

As blue light filled the air and energy crackled, the demon shot up, too stunned to grasp what was happening or to resist. Before it had a chance to even scream, it evaporated like smoke.

The final cultist was upon me then, enraged and frenzied by the loss of the others. He howled and wailed, launching a barrage of punches and slashes. I dodged as best I could, but I was being pummeled. I had to fight dirty. I kicked out with vigor, my foot connecting with the cultist's knee and breaking it. He collapsed in a howling heap. I leaped upon him and grabbed the front of his robe, then shoved my free hand hard against his face. In a matter of moments, the demon was pushed from its host, to evaporate like the others.

Gasping from injuries and exertion, I stepped over the last cultist and centered myself to face the fortune teller.

But to my bewilderment, she was gone.

I slumped to my knees for a moment, attempting to regain my thoughts and my breath. The fortune teller was on the run, probably fleeing when she saw her allies overwhelmed. Disappointing, but I could not ponder on that right now. I might have defeated these demoniacs, but I'd still lost. The Thirteenth Pentacle had Victoria, and now they possessed the complete armor too—because of me.

If I did not act by the following midnight, they were going to sacrifice my childhood friend.

I was alone, injured, and afraid.

And I was all out of ideas.

CHAPTER 10

Provoking the Pentacle

LONDON

October 31

I collapsed inside the doorway of the Evening Star sometime in the late-morning hours. Battered and bleeding, I gave Edgar quite a start, which while under normal circumstances might have proved amusing now only emphasized the desperateness of the matter.

The old man dragged me to his apartment at the rear of the bookstore and attended to my wounds. As he did so, I strained to fill Edgar in on all I had learned and all that had transpired. It certainly was not because I had deep trust for the old man. I did not. His life was one deeply immersed in secrets and lies. No, I confided in him because I had nowhere else to turn.

I told him everything. About the Thirteenth Pentacle. The gauntlet. Sir Edward Rosemond and the Apepi-possessed fortune teller. Victoria being kidnapped as a sacrifice. All of it.

Edgar said nothing. He allowed me to rant as he peeled away my waistcoat and shirt and gently washed the lacerations across my body. These he wrapped with long strips of cloth bandages.

A wave of defeat and self-loathing swept over me. I had failed. Nicholas warned me, yet in my stubbornness, I had lost the gauntlet *and* Victoria. An overwhelming desire to curl up and accept failure fought to consume my heart.

When I had exhausted myself in self-pity and fear, Edgar spoke up.

"Life is a dark place, Grey," he said, "if we choose to see it as such. We can allow it to be hopeless, fearful, and without purpose. I lived that mindset all my life. But what if we don't choose that? What if we choose hope, courage, and victory? What if that is what the darkness fears? What if the light *is* more potent than the shadow, and when a good man chooses that, then he becomes something the dark cannot control?"

Edgar's words struck me like a bullet. I was in awe that the man who had been heralded as one of the grimmest minds of our time could have such comforting and auspicious insight.

An open-mouthed expression must have crossed my face; Edgar stood and shook his head almost abashedly. "So? What will you do now?" he asked.

I searched my knowledge and experience for any idea of my next course of action. Removing my old leather journal from my coat, I retraced my notes. Edgar was right; I must choose hope.

After skimming my entries on the Samhain ritual—what was needed and when it would be performed—I realized that a glaring piece of information was missing: *where* the ritual must be performed.

"Edgar, do any of your texts mention where the Pale King's summoning ritual has to be held?"

The old man raised one gnarled finger and hastily vanished into the bookstore. A few minutes later, he returned with one of his large, heavy tomes and, sweeping aside plates and utensils on his dining table, dropped the text with a thud.

"I seem to remember seeing something," he mumbled, flipping pages. "Ah, here! This says that the cults that have attempted the summoning in the past always performed in a place of persecution and execution of those following dark arts. Hmph. I see. A kind of unholy slap in the face to the witch hunters and inquisitors of the past."

I wrote down all Edgar read, my quill flicking rapidly. "So, a site where witches were executed?" I pondered. "How many of those are there in London?"

The old man thought for a moment. Nevermore, his raven, glided in from the bookstore and landed on the table to caw at me grumpily.

"Ay! Enough of your vulgarity!" Edgar scolded.

Nevermore went silent, hopping to the far end of the dining table to avoid punishment.

"From what I recall studying British history," the old American began, "I believe there were three major locations, although how we can narrow that down, I'm not sure."

Three locations? All could be explored, but there would be no sign of the Pentacle until they arrived shortly before midnight, and by then, it would be too late.

Blast! I thought. *Now what do I do?*

I exhaled in exasperation. "Well, what are the three sites?"

Edgar counted them off with his fingers while I wrote the sites down in my journal. "From what I recollect, there are spots in Middlesex, Lancashire, and Derby. I'm fairly certain that's correct."

"Fairly?" I questioned.

"It is! It is!" he exclaimed in a huff.

I stared at the three locales I had scribbled on my journal page. I had never been to any of these locations and therefore knew absolutely nothing about them. I pressed my hand to my forehead, unsure of the next step. If I did not discover what to do, Victoria's life would be forfeit, and the city would plummet into madness.

Middlesex, Lancashire, and Derby. Where do I go?

Then it dawned on me. Sabina. Her enigmatic prophecy of three days ago. *What was it again?* "When your heart fails, look to Lancashire." Could it be?

I had experienced the miraculous before. My very own resurrection is a supreme example. I had to take a chance and trust the Almighty to shepherd my actions.

I leaped up from the table, grabbing my clothes.

"Edgar, I know where they're going. Lancashire! It's Lancashire."

Edgar looked at an old wooden wall clock opposite the table. "Eh, well, you better hurry. Lancashire is several hours by train, and you're running out of time."

"You're right! And I have one more stop to make before I go. Thank you, Edgar!" I exclaimed as I dashed from his back apartment.

"Try not to get yourself killed!" the old man yelled after me.

I ran out of the Evening Star and hailed a cab, nearly forgetting about the throbbing pain of my wounds. There was no time to lose. I had to plan this out just right—and with haste.

The sun set while I was still aboard the train from London to Lancashire. Watching its brightness sink below the horizon and the sky turn from orange to slate gray, I could not help but wonder if Victoria was safe and unharmed. She was a tenacious woman, a trait she had carried with her since childhood. I had to trust her to be wise in word and action, careful to not provoke her captors into harming her.

I just hoped to make it in time.

The hour was late by the time I arrived in Lancashire, and even later after asking for directions to the site of the witch trials and their local history. I was fatigued from traveling, and my body ached dully from multiple injuries. I mustered my will and pressed forward. After procuring a small, horse-drawn wagon, I drove swiftly toward the site described to me and in which I knew the Thirteenth Pentacle would meet.

The rural English countryside passed by me in a haze, my attention solely on what must be done.

As in my previous encounters with the Thirteenth Pentacle, I soon found myself in an isolated, pastoral area surrounded by expansive rows of trees that cut off any view from the road. A completely remote and desolate location. I looked about, and although I saw no actual carriages, I could make out signs that many had passed this way. Multiple wheel ruts grooved the mud and high grass.

The cult was here.

Even from the road, I could see the dull glow of light above the far tree line. I had to hurry. Chances were they awaited me, and I did not want to keep them.

Abandoning my wagon, I ran into the field and cut directly into the trees. I weaved through the brush, toward the steadily growing light ahead. The closer I got to the glow, the more my discernment alerted me to a massive demonic presence. I could just make out the intensifying sound of voices ahead and knew that the ritual had already begun. I quickened my pace.

Finally, I reached the edge of the tree line and received my first clear view of what I was about to walk into.

In the clearing beyond, several dozen cloaked and masked cultists stood in a circle along its perimeter, each holding a torch. Beneath their feet lay a massive summoning circle made of thousands of white stones arrayed in a complex pattern of lines and infernal symbols. At the circle's center was Sir Edward Rosemond, again adorned in his high-priest robes and mask. His arms were raised melodramatically as he led the cult in a low, droning chant. Victoria knelt at his feet, looked exhausted, battered, and afraid.

Beside Rosemont and Victoria at the circle's epicenter was the Samhain armor, displayed and complete. It could have been my imagination, but the armor seemed to exude a strange inner light—either that, or it was merely reflecting the cultists' torches.

There was no time to waste. I had to act, regardless of the overwhelming odds stacked against me.

Taking a deep breath, I barreled forward into the line of cultists directly before me. With their backs turned, it was relatively easy to take them by surprise. I collided solidly with two of them, sending them sprawling on the grass.

One of them had apparently been armed with a rifle and dropped it when I hit him. I scooped it up and immediately began to fire at the surrounding cultists, beginning with the closest.

Chaos erupted. Many attempted to run for shelter, while others who were armed essayed to return fire.

Victoria looked up in a daze as Sir Rosemond screamed to his underlings, "No! No! Stop him, Faithful! He cannot be permitted to end the ritual!"

Shots tore up the turf around me. I fired again and again. Finally, my ammunition spent, I was forced to engage the cultists head-on.

I charged at the nearest one, who was sprinting toward me with a knife in his extended hand. Swinging the rifle hard, I connected with the man's temple and dropped him instantly. I spun and intercepted another cultist attempting to grab me from behind by swinging the rifle stock firmly into the man's legs, sending him flopping into the grass.

A bullet glanced my shoulder and whipped me around. I lost my weapon. A cultist tackled me to the ground, where I landed on my side, his weight atop me, pinning my arm under me. He flailed and punched as I tried to defend myself with only one arm.

I heard Rosemond shriek, "Yes! Subdue him! Yes!"

I struggled to get my one free arm out and about my attacker's head, but I was accosted by two more cultists. They kicked me from all sides, and I attempted to protect myself. After several kicks to my legs, one finally connected with the bandaged bullet wound on my rib cage. My breath left me as pain lanced through my body.

It only took that brief moment for the cultist to bind me in my prone and vulnerable state.

The next thing I knew, my wrists had been constrained by a thick leather cord, and I was being violently yanked to my feet. The enormous summoning circle of Pentacle cultists had regained control and composure and were dragging away the several members I had managed the slay.

My heart felt as if it were being torn in two as I beheld the look of pain and despair on Victoria's tear-soaked face. I desperately wanted to run to her and reassure her that all would be all right.

Sir Rosemond laughed. It was an uneven laugh—part madness and part panic.

"Mr. Grey, that must be one of the most desperate attempts I've ever been witness to. Our Pale King comes, and your futile actions will not stop it. We are inevitable, and you are *pathetic*."

Rosemond raised his arms once again, signaling the cultists to resume the ritual. Victoria lurched to her feet to bolt, but in vain. Rosemond clutched a fist of her golden hair and forced her to her knees once again. She let out a small squeak.

This was becoming intolerable. I could not give up. Somehow, I had to stall.

I raised my voice to Rosemond, yelling over the din of droning, cultic chants.

"How do you think this ritual came to be, Rosemond? Aren't you noticing the absence of something? Or, more specifically, some*one*?"

The two cultists gripping my arms suddenly struck me for my irreverence, and warm blood dribbled from my nose. However, through my watering eyes, I could tell from the cult leader's expression that I had gotten to him. He looked about for a moment, trying to discover to whom I was referring.

"Where's your 'fortune teller,' Rosemond?" I offered.

Rosemond became wide eyed and enraged.

"What . . . what have you done with her?!" he shrieked through gritted teeth. "You killed her!"

I forced an arrogant smile. "Oh no, I didn't get that pleasure. But it would have been better for you if I had."

"What are you going on about?"

"Your guide from the Pale King, your emissary—she's not dead. She abandoned you."

Rosemond's face contorted into a mask of confusion tinged with fear.

"What the devil are you saying?"

"Your emissary has left you, Rosemond. She fled because you've failed!" I lied. To be honest, I had no real clue where the Apepi demon inside the fortune teller had run to, much less why she fled. But I would continue to bluff as long as possible.

"No! No, that cannot be! I have done everything correctly! I have always served my Lord Samhain obediently!" Rosemond was panicking, his composure starting to fray.

My two captors shifted uncomfortably as the chanting around us faltered.

I pushed Rosemond harder.

"Give up this ludicrous ritual. Can't you see it's for nothing? You've lost the Pale King's favor! His emissary has forsaken this cult! You have lost!"

Sir Rosemond screamed in terror and rage. He tugged Victoria to her feet by her hair, and she screamed as well, reaching back to where he gripped her.

"No! This is not over! We will make the sacrifice to our Lord! We will cut down this pathetic child and offer her lifeblood upon the balefire! Samhain will be pleased!"

The mad cult leader reached within his robes and retrieved a long, thin dagger, then raised it with a quivering hand to Victoria's throat. She tried to pull back from its point, but Rosemond kept her in place. Four cultists stepped from the circle, lit torches in their hands, and moved to join their fanatical chief at the center.

"Our master will have no choice but to accept this most delectable of sacrifices! And when her lifeblood drips to the earth and then is mingled with the balefire, the Pale King will honor us with his terrible coming!" Rosemond bellowed.

He began to press the dagger's point to Victoria's neck. Her panicked eyes stared fixedly into mine. At that moment, everything slipped away, and all I could see was my childhood friend—my only friend—whom I had left behind.

"No!" I screamed.

A thunderous clap filled the night. Everyone present froze in uncertainty and confusion.

Slowly, one of the torch-bearing cultists slumped heavily to the ground.

"Wha—" Rosemond began but was cut off by another loud crack.

Another cultist with a torch fell.

Then, all at once, dozens and dozens of cracks resounded, and I realized, as did my captors, that gunfire had erupted all around us. The cult scattered, some turning and returning fire toward the surrounding tree line, while many others simply ran, screaming, for their lives.

Within moments, men began pouring out of the blackness, many wearing constables' uniforms but all brandishing firearms and exchanging fire with the Thirteenth Pentacle.

The two cultists holding me in place stumbled about, disconcerted, their gazes whipping all around in terror, and I seized the opportunity. With my hands still bound behind me, I lunged forward, throwing my body weight into the one with his back to me and sending him sprawling on his face. The second cultist dashed toward me to regain control but was abruptly struck down by a gunshot.

I looked to find the source of the shot, only to see Sir Nicholas Grey, my brother, striding up to me with a pistol in one hand and a saber in the other.

"Turn around," he grunted.

I obeyed, and he cut away my bonds with his saber.

"Did you perhaps do some sightseeing on the way here?" I asked, rubbing my wrists and turning to face him. "It took you long enough."

"It took us longer to locate you than I thought. Next time, give better directions."

I turned toward the center of the circle, where last I saw Rosemond and Victoria. There, amidst the chaos, Victoria wrestled violently with the deranged Rosemond for the dagger. Rosemond's mask had been torn away, and he bared his teeth hatefully at the woman who dared to defy him.

"I'll get Rosemond!" I yelled at Nicholas, then erupted into a sprint toward the grappling pair. Ducking and weaving through the ocean of fighting bodies, I swung and punched and dove as best I could manage, in a rush to reach the overpowered Victoria. I imagined her quickly falling prey to the bigger man, who, although much her elder, was empowered by his rage and madness.

Suddenly the pair broke apart, Rosemond still in possession of the knife. Victoria stumbled backward, and the lunatic raised the blade high, intent on piercing her through. She brought her hands up to shield herself as the knife fell. But just as it might have struck her down, I dove into her, taking the knife's bite in the shoulder blade. We toppled to the ground together.

At that same moment, a shot rang out. Sir Rosemond screamed out in agony and surprise.

My body atop Victoria to shield her, I asked, "Are you hurt?"

She stared up at me, teary and breathless. "No. I almost had him, though, didn't I?"

I could not help but smile.

"Yes. You very nearly did, at that."

My brother's loud, abrasive voice interrupted. "Asher! Rosemond's escaping!"

I pushed myself up to spot the elderly madman stumbling off into the darkness of the nearby trees. Breaking into pursuit, I yelled over my shoulder, "I'm going after him! See to Victoria!"

I blindly felt my way through the black underbrush, the echoes of gunfire and shouting falling behind me. Ahead of me, I could just make out the cult leader staggering through the foliage. I followed the sounds, gaining on him, close enough now to hear the whispers of Rosemond talking to himself.

After several minutes in pursuit, with branches slapping me in the face, I abruptly burst into a still, open clearing. Illuminated by moonlight, I saw Sir Rosemond crossing to the far side, limping from my brother's bullet.

"That's enough, Rosemond!" I shouted. "There's no point in fleeing. It's over!"

The leader of the Thirteenth Pentacle turned back to face me. In the moonlight, I saw the desperation on his face, the look of a cornered animal.

"Grey," he spat, "you believe this is over? Truly? I will return with even more followers. And when I do, the Pale King will return in balefire! He will see and know that I was faithful! And *you*, and your pathetic city, will lament in witness to the favor upon me!"

"Favor?" a voice rasped from just behind a Rosemond.

He turned, alarmed, as a figure emerged from the tree line.

The fortune teller. Even from a distance, I saw the eyes of the white-haired woman glowing a pale red in the gloom. My discernment screamed. It was clear that the Apepi demon within the woman was the one doing the talking.

"What favor do you believe you have?" it asked.

"You," Rosemond stammered. "You left us. Left *me*! Why?"

The woman tilted her head to the side.

"It was apparent that you were not the one to bring the Pale King to this plane. Like all men in authority, your only concern was your ambitions and name. You're not worthy. You never were."

Rosemond was flabbergasted. "What?"

The fortune teller stepped past him, facing me with her back to the old man.

"You were no match for the Rekindled One. He's made a fool of you and your pitiful group of followers," she said, all the while staring at me. "We gave you the ritual. We gave you the components. Still you could not succeed."

"Wait, no!" Rosemond yelled. "It's not my fault! If I had more men! More time!"

The woman shook her head.

"No. This endeavor has been a failure. *Your* failure."

Suddenly, from beyond the tree line spilled dozens of shapes. Inhuman shapes.

I knew instantly that they were demons. They crept out of the trees, large black silhouettes standing all about Rosemond. They seemed solid and yet not solid, as if the shadows themselves had taken on shape and substance. They exuded such repulsion that I could barely stand to look at them.

Rosemond's face turned white as a corpse. He tried to scream, but pure terror stole his voice. He turned the fortune teller. "No! No, please! I served! I was faithful!"

The woman tilted her head again.

"Edward Rosemond, you made a deal. You agreed to serve the Pale King and bring him into this world in exchange for your very soul. You have failed to meet your end of the bargain. The Pale King is not wont to respond lightly to failure. Do you know what kind of king he is?"

I knew what was about to happen and was horrified. Disgust filled my heart and reached my stomach, leaving me queasy. I could not watch it. But I could not look away. All I could do was whisper the answer.

"The mighty and terrible," I breathed.

In a violent flash, the black, demonic shapes rushed upon Rosemond, clawing and gnashing. He attempted to struggle, but it was fruitless. The infernal creatures dragged the poor fool away into the dark as he kicked and begged and unleashed one last, pathetic, gurgling scream.

Then, a few seconds later, he was gone, and all was silent once again.

I was alone with the fortune teller.

She gave a slight smile, slowly backing away. "You *are* an interesting one, Asher Grey. As I told you before, we have, and will, continue to observe you with great interest."

The woman's face turned toward the trees, and then she vanished as well, leaving only her hiss: "Farewell, Asher Grey. We will see each other again."

EPILOGUE

It took several grueling weeks for Scotland Yard to make sense of all that had transpired and what was truly attempted by the Thirteenth Pentacle on All Hallows' Eve.

Thanks to some keen political manipulations by Sir Nicholas, the news of a "hellfire club" so influential that it counted aristocrats and Parliament members amongst its ranks never reached the public's ears. The story released about Sir Edward Rosemond was of an unfortunate accident while on holiday in the forest of Lancashire. It simply would not benefit the empire to have a scandal within the quarters of Whitehall.

My brother did not believe my story, of course—that Rosemond was quite literally dragged off to Hell by demons. He was not a little incensed when I would not budge from that account but begrudgingly dropped the subject, especially after a search of the forested area yielded no trace of the old man.

He did thank me, in his way, for reaching out to him and Scotland Yard that evening before I rushed off to Lancashire. Thankfully, I had managed to stall the cultists long enough for backup to reach us in time.

Nicholas also informed me, some months later, that Her Majesty was aware of the general happenings of that evening and was—how did he put it?—"in my debt."

To be honest, I'm not quite sure how I feel about that.

Regardless, Lady Victoria Kaylock was returned home safely from what sources said at the time was a kidnapping incident. Scotland

Yard took the credit for her safe return, of course.

About a week after the affair on All Hallows' Eve, Victoria performed, as scheduled, at Her Majesty's Theatre as Brünnhilde in Wagner's *Twilight of the Gods*. I was in attendance.

Victoria's performance was quite good, and although I know little of musical theater, I thought her voice sublime. Regardless of the disreputable reputations of opera singers, she sang with a confidence that was inspiring. Later that evening, after her performance, I met up with her at Wendell's once again. This time without Lady Pemberton, to my delight.

"How have you been recovering?" I asked her.

"Oh, those bumps and scratches were hardly noticeable," she said dismissively. "Besides, it's nothing the makeup department can't cover up before a performance."

It was true. She seemed none the worse for wear, with hardly a noticeable mark in view. She looked clean and beautiful, as always.

"Ash," she whispered to me, fidgeting with her coffee cup.

"Hmm?"

"You do hear me when I say that I know you did not steal mother's broach back then, don't you?"

I sighed. "Yes. I know you believe me."

Victoria shook her head.

"No. I said I *know* you didn't. I mean . . . I . . . Oh, just look here."

Reaching into her handbag, Victoria removed a round, bright-blue broach. One I remembered all too well.

I was stunned. "I don't understand."

Victoria looked at me intensely, melancholy reflected in her eyes.

"About three years after you left, the second-floor servant discovered this amongst my mother's old things."

"Wait. Your *mother's*?"

Victoria nodded sadly. "Father was furious, but also ashamed. He accused you, threatened you and your family. And all along, my mother . . ." She drifted into silence.

So that was it, then. Lady Kaylock had staged the theft to rid her daughter's life of me. I had been framed.

"Ash, I am so sorry," Victoria whispered.

I should've felt anger at that moment, or perhaps bitterness. But I did not. Something had happened to me in this case, something I could not have foreseen. And although I was slow to admit it, my heart was different somehow.

I lightly rested my hand on Victoria's.

"It's okay. There's no reason to be sorry. We're here now. That's the important thing."

Victoria looked at me with tear-filled eyes, an expression of joy filling her face.

Awkwardly, I withdrew my hand.

"Shall we get another pot of coffee?" I asked, clearing my throat.

"Yes! And then we can talk about our next case!" she said excitingly as she slid the brooch back into her bag.

I raised my eyebrows.

"*Our* next case?"

"Of course! You can't forget all the assistance I have given you. Where would you be without me?"

"Is that right?"

"It is! Now, what is it? Ghosts? A witch? Possession? Don't hold back, Ash. We're in this together. You need me!"

As Victoria went on and on in bubbly excitement, I attempted to invent an excuse as to why she couldn't aid me on my cases.

I mean, having Victoria join me in my career would be absurd. Wouldn't it?

www.ingramcontent.com/pod-product-compliance
Lightning Source LLC
LaVergne TN
LVHW092050060526
838201LV00047B/1328